SHE'S YOURS NOW

PETER. A. FULKER

SHE'S YOURS NOW
PETER. A. FULKER

ISBN 9781914615788
A CIP catalogue record for this
book is available from the British Library.

Published 2023
Tricorn Books,
Treadgolds
1a Bishop Street
Portsmouth
PO1 3HN

SHE'S YOURS NOW

Contents

DEDICATIONS
Absolutely to my little Gladys, the only opinion
I seek and that means everything to me.
Thank you for your encouragement and
patience, we are nearly there.

And to her friend Karen cos I said I would.

CHAPTER ONE (MY EXPERIENCE!)

Although it may be difficult to believe the events that follow, they did actually happen; they are my story and I did live through it. You may choose to dismiss the whole thing as a fantasy. I sometimes, even now, find it difficult to comprehend and I know the truth. So I will just ask that you remember one thing. That the mind cannot begin to work unless it's open. Bear this in mind and, as you read my story, try to open yours and not dismiss what I say, because I personally know what is true, although I cannot always explain it.

My story begins on a warm spring morning in Barnes, which is a leafy London suburb on the banks of the Thames. Although being just eight miles from the centre of London's theatre land, it somehow still manages to retain a village atmosphere, being bordered on one side by the river and on the other by the common, complete with a pond, fashionable twee pubs and probably a thousand acres of woods, sports fields, and even boasting its own orchard. It was one of those mornings that makes you take your jacket off because you can feel the warmth on your back. I was filled with optimism, a new summer is nearly here, you feel great, nothing could possibly go wrong. How could I be so wrong? With this overwhelming feeling of well-being bathing me like a warm bath, I strolled to work, through the shady canopy of trees across Barnes common, not a care, you could say full of the joys of spring in anticipation of the days ahead. God certainly has a weird sense of humour I have always felt and still do feel that most of us are never more than a heartbeat away from a major life-changing incident; the majority of us travel through life never knowing how close we were to catastrophe on numerous occasions.

My first recollection of the events that warm spring day was seeing her walking toward me. There were many people around but none seemed to register. If called on I could not describe any of them. My eyes and my attention just focused on her for some reason, which remains unexplained, but I've come to terms with it in my own way as time has passed. She was, I remember thinking, probably in her late thirties, on the tall side, without doubt stunning.

But as a contented married and more or less faithful man – although I must stress that I am, like most men, not oblivious to noticing attractive women – this was different.

It was not a sexual thing but I was just uncontrollably drawn to her eyes. She looked straight at me as if drawing me in. There was a slight, perhaps enigmatic smile on her face as though it was all part of some plan that only she was privy to and I was merely drawn in, unable to exercise any control.

Perhaps this is just my mind trying, retrospectively, to make some sense of it. I can only relay my feelings and hope for the truth.

Then she was passed and I was shaking my head as if trying to wake up from a dream. I made myself look forward and not turn my head to follow her. I knew subconsciously that there was something strange happening, a feeling of unease had come over me, like a cold chill.

I walked on with this feeling for a few seconds. I was conscious of an almighty screech of brakes followed by a loud bang, people screaming, all the unmistakable noises that went with what I already knew involved her.

Turning slowly, I took in the scene, everything I had felt, was before me. She lay on her side to one side of the road, completely still and unmoving. I moved as quickly as I could to her. I knelt down, turned her to try to see what sort of damage had occurred and got her in the recovery position. I expected blood and substantial gore, but I couldn't see anything; it appeared to all intents and purposes that she was just sleeping. Perhaps my mind was just seeing what it wanted to see, but I still don't recall any physically visible damage.

I glanced up looking for a vehicle. Although I hadn't witnessed the impact, I knew there had been one, but could see nothing.

By now, people were crowding around, ambulances had been summoned and the police were arriving.

"Are you with her sir?"

I could vaguely hear someone talking, but I didn't seem to be functioning as I should. I could not detect any signs of life but knew I had to persevere. To this day I've no idea why but I've learnt not to question some things. This from the world's biggest sceptic.

Suddenly I felt her hands gripping me high up on my arms, the heat was tremendous and pulsed through my body. I felt like shouting in pain but couldn't. My head was buzzing, like a tape playing at fantastic speed, I could, by now, hear nothing, see nothing and now feel nothing. Then I could hear over and over in my head, "She's yours now, she's yours now, help her."

I could now see the scene all there before me, the ambulance crew, the police, the full spectrum of human detritus that gathers to the scene of any or anybody's misfortune.

Slowly as my brain seemed to start to function and begin to rationalise events more normally, a thought struck me, it coincided with one of the policemen saying, "This one's bloody fainted, he wasn't hit, was he?"

Jesus bloody Christ, that's me they are talking about,

the bloke that's fainted, ME an ex-marine, a rugby player, I don't faint!

The thought now struck me. How the bloody hell can I see all this? I tried to calm myself down and analyse what was happening, but I have to admit to being very close to utter bloody panic.

Right, now think. It was very hard I can tell you. But this is what I remember. I could look down on all that was happening. Yes, I was above the whole thing like what people describe as an out of body experience of some kind, something I'd spent my whole life belittling.

But I was trying to behave calmly and keep panic at bay. I could look, see and hear everything, I could even see me lying there. I remember wondering if perhaps I was dead.

I didn't feel dead, I couldn't see any reason why I could possibly have been dead, so this train of thought disappeared, dismissed as ridiculous which, given the circumstances in itself is faintly absurd.

"She's gone," one of the paramedics informed the police. "Nothing we could do, I'm afraid."

"What about this one?" And they turned their attention to me.

"Oh he's all right, he'll be round in a minute, just fainted." "I've not bloody fainted." Christ, I was back!

"But I did feel a bit strange."

"Yes sir, felt a bit strange, went unconscious. That's what we in the police call fainting."

Just then a young constable came up to the sergeant.

"No one can identify the car sir, just a big one, that's it sorry."

"All right son, keep trying."

"How are you feeling now sir?" He addressed to me, having had a few minutes to get myself together.

I mumbled, "I'm OK thanks." I was anything but, but even in my state of complete shock realised that to give this sergeant even a clue as to what was going on in my head was a direct route to being sectioned or something equally unpleasant.

They seemed to lose interest in me somewhat with all that was going on, which suited me. The more time I had to try and make some sense of what had happened in the last few minutes the better.

Which was a forlorn hope because even though I've learnt to accept it, I still can't explain it.

I was now at least on my feet and more or less in control of my emotions, thinking on my feet as I've always thought was my forte.

"You can't leave sir." The sergeant had noticed my recovery. "We need a statement."

"Yes I understand that," I retorted. "Here's my card, my office is that building just over there."

We all turned to look at my office, which is a converted GPO sorting warehouse, about two hundred yards away. Part of a group of listed buildings all been restored, very nice and very sought after. Very Barnes.

"I am going straight there now, so when you're finished up here come over have a coffee and I'll give you everything I know."

Some bloody chance! I think the offer of a free cup of coffee and a nice sit down was too much to refuse.

"All right sir, we should be there within an hour."

"Fine, I'll see you then," I acknowledged. Then I was away like an athlete. I needed to get to familiar ground, I still felt like I'd been knocked over, even though my senses were returning. I was afraid to even contemplate recent events. I think subconsciously I was just desperately trying to get to familiar ground where I hoped my head and myself could begin to get back in control.

CHAPTER TWO (REALISATION)

I felt an enormous sense of relief as I passed through my office door. This was my world, my own little empire where I could feel safe. I remember the feeling of renewed confidence as soon as I entered the building – this was what I needed. My name, by the way, is David Hollins and this is my company DHN. Which, with a distinct lack of imagination, stands for David Hollins News. We are a news agency, small but very good. We find or pursue any and all stories for most daily newspapers.

There are just six of us in the company; as I said, small, but I think the best. We certainly have got ourselves a top reputation, which makes us very successful. How did I get from the military to this? Well on leaving the marines I went to university, reading journalism, got my degree, worked as a reporter for some time and sort of just moved on to the agency. I always wanted to be the boss, knew I could never afford to buy a newspaper, but had a large circle of friends in the press and always felt I was good at what I did. Being naturally nosy of course was the most important asset.

I am now thirty-eight and have run the agency for six years and love every minute I'm here.

I entered the main office with a crash, throwing the door open so it impacted loudly against the nearest desk, trying to convince myself that I was in control I suppose.

"Bloody hell, what happened to you? You look bloody awful."

That was Mike Denby, my number two.

"I'll tell you later, right now I need you in my office,

12

RIGHT NOW!"I could sense the eyes turned in my direction, all curious as to what the problem was. I let him in to my office, closing the door behind him. "Take a seat," I said, settling into mine.

I was writing furiously. "Right. I want you to do something for me."

Mike looked at me with a quizzical frown, obviously my behaviour was not as normal as I thought.

"OK boss, what?"

I passed my scribblings over the desk. "I want everything, and I mean everything on these. The car, Lady Sarah Benson, Lord Gordon Benson, her daughter Maggie, Margaret obviously, and his other children, three I think. That's the car registration number and I'm pretty sure it's a Bentley Continental Park Ward."

Mike's jaw was hanging open now. "How come that you, who doesn't know a Ford Focus from a Rolls Royce, suddenly recognises a Park Ward Continental?"

"One day I might tell you, but for now just do it and it's just between me and you, OK?"

"Fine," he said as he walked out the door. That's what makes Mike invaluable, no questions, no discussions, he just gets it done.

Mary bought me a cup of tea. Mary, early twenties, dark, very attractive, is admin, a title which does her a disservice. All offices have a Mary, if they're lucky. She runs everything, without her we would cease to function. I've tried to promote her, but she won't have it.

"I'm happy where I am thanks" so I pay her over the odds and hope we keep her happy. There is one small fly in the ointment however. She has, how can I put it, a very relaxed attitude to morals, which is a source of endless entertainment in the office but does sometimes cause us problems – wives,

13

boyfriends, partners, etc. Turning up at the office, tantrums, scenes, you get the idea. But at the end of the day, she is loved by everyone here and irreplaceable.

Sipping my tea, inevitably I started to analyse what had happened in the last couple of hours without too much success. If I could have found some way of denying what had happened, I would have jumped at it, but there were things I could not ignore.

The fact that I had given Mike the Bentley registration number, even though I had never seen the car that had killed her. Oh yes, I knew it had been the car that had killed her without doubt. I had given him her and her husband's names, these were yet to be confirmed, but I knew beyond any doubt that they would be. The fact that I had given him the names of the children and, I noted that I called the daughter Maggie, and described her as Sarah's daughter when I knew Gordon Benson was her father. I knew I was relaying Sarah's thoughts, that she had dismissed Gordon as the father and this was why I wrote it in that way.

Can you imagine how difficult this was for me, the biggest sceptic ever, my whole life had been facts. I had always felt nothing but scorn for anything supernatural or mystical in any form. I even find that quite hard to write.

But the facts were there right in front of me; facts, facts that I couldn't ignore however inconvenient they were.

There was a knock on the door. Mary put her head round. "Inspector Densil and Sergeant Millar, they say you are expecting them."

'Yes, show them in could you, and could you sort tea, coffee, biscuits?"

"All arranged," she said rather curtly, feeling I know that my suggesting she needed reminding of her office duties was a mild insult. I must try harder!

"Come in, come in, please take a seat."

"Thank you sir," said Inspector Densil as they both took a seat.

"Please, Dave, David or even Mr Hollins if you want to be formal, but not sir please."

"OK Mr Hollins."

So we proceeded. They asked me what I saw, whether I knew her, all answered in the negative. Our tea and coffee arrived with a lovely plate of assorted biscuits, which the sergeant and inspector made the most of. I must learn not to doubt Mary! I had already noted the look that Mary had given to Sergeant Millar and felt a twinge of sympathy for the poor man; he had no idea what a force our Mary was. Still, not my problem hopefully!"Why did you go straight over to her then Mr Hollins?" asked the sergeant.

"You were not the nearest, in fact you were quite a distance." There was a pause.

"Was I? I'd no idea, I just reacted quicker I suppose, military training probably."I felt quite proud, at last I was reacting like my normal self. "What about you sergeant? You're ex-military, are you not?"

"Well, eh, yes I am. How did you know?"

"It takes one to know one, or so they say, right?" I said.

"Eh yes, very true sir."

"Please, not sir Sergeant."

He made his apologies but had lost any dominance he'd had in this interview. We went over everything that had happened a few times more.

They obviously believed that I knew her, but couldn't see how I fitted in, I was after all a pedestrian and not with her at the time of the incident. I think it was just their instinct for someone who may not be lying, but was, at least, not telling everything.

Eventually, having had their fill of tea and biscuits and having frustrated themselves not being able to figure out my part in all this, they stood up ready to leave.

"We will very likely need to talk to you again, sir."

"Fine Inspector, any time, you know where I am, best to ring just so I can get the kettle and biscuits organised."

Mary had already grabbed the sergeant by his arm and was leading him off towards the exit deep in conversation. The poor man. He still had no clue what was happening.

"Well goodbye for now, sir."

"Oh yes Inspector, be seeing you," I said.

I'd just settled in my chair when there was a soft knock followed by Mike entering. He didn't look too happy. When you've worked together as long as us two you recognise every look and mood. I thought it best to leave it, he wouldn't be capable of holding back for long and I'd get it full blast pretty soon. Mike was a couple of years younger than me, tall, blond and handsome. I had grabbed him when I started the agency; although he was really very young, I could see his potential and he proved me right over and over.

"It's the information you asked for. Well all I've got so far."

"Sit down Mike." I gestured to his normal chair, and he sat down. There was a pause while I waited for him to start.

"Mike," I started.

"Look Dave, these people that you're looking into, the Bensons."

"Yes, what about them?"

"Let me give you the information I've got first, then we can talk."

"Fair enough," I said, happy now that his worries were going to be forthcoming.

He tossed a folder over the desk. I opened it up and started to read.

After a few minutes he spoke.

"As you can see, the Bensons own the world, not literally of course but they are extremely rich and of course powerful, everything from offshore exploration, electronics, engineering and arms, you name it they have interests somewhere.

"Old man Benson, Lord Benson, died three or four months ago, nothing suspicious, cancer.

"The oldest son Nigel has taken over the business interests, also is using the title, I'm not sure he is entitled but he's doing it anyway! "The other offspring, Jonathan and Camilla, are nothing really, just your average rich spoilt parasites always in trouble, and bailed out by Daddy and now big brother.

"There is something which might be of interest concerning Lady Benson." He paused.

"Well," I said, "Let's have it." He took a deep breath and continued. "Lord Benson the elder was married, and as far as the information we've been able to obtain so far, he doesn't appear to have ever been divorced. This will all be verified in the fullness of time of course, but at present it seems accurate. The girl was a Sarah Conway, up-and-coming model of the time, about eighteen. He was then, I don't know, about thirty-eight or thirty-nine, already very rich and already a real bastard."

I poured him a cup of tea, not that I thought he needed one but I could see him getting more tense with every word and thought a break would ease his mood somewhat.

He took a mouthful and was off again. "I'm just getting to the interesting bits." I sat back and let him go. "They were together for about three years when our girl appears to have upped and done a runner, disappeared without a trace." Another pause.

"So?" I said.

"Oh yeah. Now the old man searched or at least hired people to search, to no avail. But my sources reckon that the search has restarted! Now, I'm thinking, bearing in mind you mentioned a daughter of which there is no record, so I don't know where you got that from? So maybe – and it's a big maybe – our Lady Sarah was with child when she fled, the said child could be eighteen now, and the only reason I can think of for the search to resume after all these years ... well there are several reasons I can think of.

"One, the old man left a will and left Lady S. a sizeable chunk. Two, he knew of the offspring and left both of them a good slice of the pie."

I took a mouthful of my tea.

"Well done Mike," I said.

"No wait, I've not finished," said Mike.

"Firstly, why do they want to find Lady S. and the kid? To buy them off? To let them know of their good fortune? I tell you what I think, it's to get rid of them!"

I asked him what bought him to this conclusion. I did feel it was a big leap from thinking we were dealing with the unpleasant, to murdering their close family. Anyway, finally we arrived at what had been bothering him all along.

"You remember my friend Sean? My roomy at university?"

Of course I remembered, he wasn't just a mate, Mike was his best man, he was godfather to his son, they were like brothers.

"Yes of course I remember him."

"Well if you remember, Mike was killed, hit and run, he'd just picked up his son from school," he paused. I could see the emotion this caused, I could feel his pain, but I knew he needed to speak the words. I had a feeling where this was heading as well.

"They mowed them down, both of them, what sort of people could do that? They were killed instantly. At least that's what we were told, I hope it's true." The tears were flowing now. I didn't speak, I knew he needed time to control these emotions which even with the passage of time were just beneath the surface. So we just sat for a while in complete silence.

"What I've never said, at least not out loud, was that when this happened, as you know he was a journalist." I nodded. He still wasn't ready for chat.

"Well when it happened he was investigating the Bensons! He told me just the day before. It was something to do with deals with Saddam Hussein.

"What, I never found out, but Sean thought that they had found out he was nosing around and he told me, 'It's the old man and the son Nigel, I'm sure I'm being followed, they are ruthless, the more I find out the more I'm worried.'

"Of course my retort was 'Piss off you big Jessie'. He then grabbed me by the throat.

'I'm not fucking joking Mike, promise you'll look after Jakie and Sam should anything happen.' He was shaking Dave, I remember it like yesterday.

"The next day they were dead, that's how I had all this stuff ready to give you, I've been gathering what I could for years. It's not easy, they cover themselves in every way and nobody will say a word, completely petrified, what can you do?" He was back to his old self again. "Why did you never say anything, Mike?" I said.

"Maybe I would if I could have got something concrete, but the secrecy that surrounds them is unbelievable."

"Well perhaps we have got some inside information, Mike."

"What the bloody hell do you mean?" He said.

"Look Mike," I said, "I'm going to tell you something and I don't want you to say a word until I'm finished, just sit quietly, otherwise I won't be able to finish."

He gave me a quizzical sort of look, but said, "Not a word," and settled back to listen.

Then it poured out, the whole afternoon, the woman, the car, the police, and of course my experience. I sat back.

"Well?" I said.

Another pause. "Fucking hell." Was this good or bad? I waited and waited.

"Fucking hell!"

"I already got that bit, could we move on?"

"Well that's great, so how does this knowledge manifest itself?

Do you know it all straight away or does it come in waves?"

Well at least he wasn't questioning my sanity, in fact he seemed to accept it all without any problem. I gave it a bit of thought. "I don't really know, some things I just know, some things come to me when I'm asked. Like, I know for sure that Sarah and Maggie, her daughter Margaret actually, have been living in Spain. I even know the village. Also I know that if questioned I could answer in fluent

Spanish."

"How can you possibly know that?" said Mike.

"I don't bloody know, I just do," was all I could say.

"Well bloody fucking fucking hell."

"I think we've done that bit Mike."

"Look boss, the way I see it is, don't question what we can't possibly explain, just thank God and take full advantage. You gleaned more facts in a few minutes flying around the common with a bloody ouija board under your arm, than I managed in years."

"I never had …"

"I know, I know, I'm not speaking literally but metaphorically.

But you see my point, we must take full advantage. For the first time we might be able to get these bastards."I could of course see his point. They had probably killed not only Sarah but Mike's friend Sean and of course his lad Jake, and I could see what this still meant to Mike.

"Did you then, Mike?"

"Did I what?"

"Did you look after Sean's wife Sammie?"

Mike looked shocked and actually started blushing. "Yeah, well you know I see a lot of her, make sure she's all right and that."

"Does she know how you feel about her?" I asked quietly. "What on earth do you mean? There is nothing going on between us …"

"That's not what I asked mate, but forget it for now, we'll come back to it when our present predicament is sorted out."

He didn't answer. I could see it was a sensitive area for him so decided to leave it alone.

"Just one thing I'd like to say Mike, that's thanks, thanks for not laughing at me, thanks for not dismissing me as a loony and thanks for being a good friend, and I really mean that Mike. I don't mind telling you that there have been a few times today when I began to doubt myself.

"I've known you a long time Dave and I know when you're joking and when it's serious and I didn't doubt you for a second."

"Right, what now?" said Mike.

"I mean, now we've got all that b-shit out of the way!"

"We'll phone his lordship and see if we can put the cat among the pigeons."

"What number?" said Mike

I wrote furiously on a piece of paper and handed it to Mike.

"01428, that's Surrey!" I shot him an irritated look. "OK I'm on it."

Another example of knowing things I had no right to have any clue about, also having to write it to be accurate, not just out of my head. I was getting more accepting of the situation and began to feel that I would become more adept at using this ... what, gift, power, god knows what it was, but I've got it and I was beginning to feel that I had some sort of duty to find out why, and act appropriately, whatever that may turn out to be.

Mike came back into the office waving the phone. "He won't talk to me, wants the boss."

"Does he indeed?" I took the phone.

"Hello sir, David Hollins here."

"Who the bloody hell is David whoever you are and how did you get my private number?"

I paused.

"Firstly, am I talking to Lord Benson junior?" I was trying to inject sarcasm to needle him.

"Of course it is, who else would you get on this number? And it's Lord Benson, not junior."

His anger was obvious in his voice, which was very satisfying.

"Where did you get this number anyway, it's strictly exclusive."

"Well sir, I was actually given it by your stepmother ..."

Now that's what you call a pregnant pause.

"You what? She's dead, well as far as we know, nobody's heard from her for years."

He had slipped up and he knew it and was desperately

trying to recover.

"So when did you meet? And how was she? And again who the bloody hell are you?"

He blustered, trying to recover.

"Right sir, I'm David Hollins, as I said, of David Hollins News. What I would like to do is come and see you, so we can discuss this face to face."

"When did you want to come?"

"As soon as possible, perhaps tomorrow morning?"

He was so desperate to find out what, if anything, I knew.

He was rattled, I could hear it and feel it in every word.

"OK tomorrow morning about eleven, we can have a drink and a chat, and if you see Sarah in the meantime, give her the family's best wishes."

Don't think I'll fall for that shit, you bastard.

"Yes that's fine, I'll look forward to it sir, until then Lord Benson." And I put the phone down.

"Well," said Mike who'd been listening on the speaker phone.

"He was shitting his pants."

"That's just what I thought," I said, "and he's going to have a lot more to worry about before we've finished with him."

"So what now till we go to Surrey?" said Mike.

"I shall go home. I told you and now I've got someone else to tell."

I had already made the decision to tell my wife Caroline the full story. Her and Mike were two of the people that meant the most to me; there was no way I could ever keep a thing like this a secret.

CHAPTER THREE (TWO WOMEN)

I arrived home having done the short walk home in about fifteen minutes. I had of course to pass right by the spot where the accident had taken place, well not an accident, a murder. It made me realise, all that had happened, and yet it was only six or seven hours since I left my house this morning. I paused to examine the scene where it had happened.

"It makes you wonder, doesn't it?"

I looked around, assuming someone had walked up behind me. There was not a sign of anyone within fifty metres.

"Who's that?"

"It's me, who do you think it is?"

"Who the bloody hell is Me!?"

I already had a creeping feeling in my head and it began to move down my neck and followed on down my back.

"It's Sarah, well Lady Sarah if I'm really honest."

"But you're …"

"Dead, yes I know, bit of a puzzle isn't it, so don't ask me anything about what's going on, cos I'm new to all this as you know."

"Listen Sarah, I'm sorry but I'm not going through all that, your ladyship crap."

"I quite understand David. It'll take us a while to get used to the protocol, if there is any."

"I don't intend to get used to anything," I said in a voice loud enough to start attracting attention. "Look, just leave it till later, I need time to sort all this out. Sarah, can you hear me?"

"OK I'll talk to you later."

And she was gone. I don't know how I knew but I just did.
I entered through my front door.

"ANYONE HOME?" I shouted.

"Caz, you there?" Caz was my wife. Caroline to be accurate but Caz was just my nickname for her.

"Yes I'm here, just coming. You're early," she said as she appeared, walking down the stairs.

She looked at me quizzically. "What's the problem? Do you want to talk?" She obviously could tell something was worrying me.

"I think we should, is now OK?"

She took my hand and said, "Yes now is fine," and led me into the kitchen.

We sat down. She said nothing, knowing I suppose that I would tell her as soon as I was ready.

It was a few moments, then it all came pouring out, everything except the talking to a corpse, I couldn't quite come to terms with this myself yet, so I still needed some time. The woman, the car, the crash, the police, and finally of course, my experience! I still couldn't figure out how to describe what happened, but I felt so much better telling Caz. Even though I held back the chatting to the dead.

Her curious look had been replaced by a sort of bemused grin.

She looked straight at me and said, "You're not starting to find men attractive are you?"

I must have looked shocked.

"I'm sorry sweetheart, I couldn't resist it."

I looked serious.

"Just listen, I don't fancy men, I don't want to wear your clothes and I won't be wearing your knickers any day soon." I put my arms around her and we kissed long and lovingly, not as a prelude to anything but just to tell me everything

25

was OK and that she understood what I was feeling. She squeezed me tightly. "Well no more than you do now!"

The lighthearted banter was just to hide the fact that she knew, instinctively knew, I was troubled, even though I did my best to hide it.

I pretended not to notice, but of course we were both aware. When couples know each other so well, know your mood, your anxieties, they don't feel the need to say anything just to hold you, just mutual comfort really. I'm a lucky man.

"One thing you must promise me, I know you are going to pursue this and I won't try to dissuade you, but you must promise me, you will take John with you tomorrow."

I had already decided to take John anyway, so it was no problem to say, "Yes of course I will."

The John in question was John Penn my former sergeant major in the marines. He had trained me and several thousand others in his twenty-to-thirty-year career. We had been in action together in Bosnia, the Gulf, the Congo and many lesser-known places all over the world. He retired before I finished and of course we lost touch. A number of years later – this was after I'd started the agency – I heard, I can't remember exactly how, but the ex-military has a grapevine second to none. I heard he was having a bad time, his wife had died suddenly and prematurely, he was hitting the bottle more than was good for him, a familiar story with old soldiers unfortunately. To cut a long story short, I looked him up, tried to make out it was coincidental, which he didn't believe for one minute but pretended to. So after drinking ourselves nearly to oblivion I managed to persuade him to work for me. I'd convinced him that the job was for real, which as it turned out once he started, I realised it was. I don't know how we ever managed without him. I knew that having agreed to the job, he would stick to it irrespective of what his feelings were.

So John joined the team and soon we all became his little troop. Apart from his duties as head of security, driver and numerous other things, which god knows what we did before he joined us, he soon became patriarch to our little band, sorting everybody's lives in more ways than I ever knew of or, probably just as well, never will. My Caz loved him like a father, and the feeling I must say was reciprocated, they formed a bond that it would take a very brave or stupid man to intrude into.

"One other thing," I said, "do you remember Mike's friend Sean who was killed with his lad Jake a few years ago?"

"Yes," she said. "Well he left a wife."

"Sammie, yes I know."

I didn't question how she knew all this but just carried on. "Well, Mike …"

"Is in love with her, of course I know," she said interrupting.

"How the bloody hell did you know that?"

"I've known for a couple of years, you only had to see them together. I don't know about you newshounds, you chase a story like lunatics all over the world, but can't see what's right in front of you."

I was gobsmacked. "How do you know her?" I asked.

"We use the same hairdresser and have coffee together regularly. In fact we are pretty good friends now."

"Does she know? About Mike, I mean?" "I'm not sure, but I don't think she would be too unhappy."

"You mean she feels the same?"

Caz thought for a while. "I'll just say this, I get the feeling that she wouldn't be upset if he opened up, instead of this constant just being friends."

Why, I thought, did I have all these computers and staff, when my wife learns more at the hairdressers! Perhaps I will never understand.

CHAPTER FOUR(THE STORY)

Come the morning I got to the office early. There was something I wasn't looking forward to but I had to do. Mike had arrived early as well so I grabbed him and ushered him into my office"What's up boss?" "Well Mike," I said, "this is very difficult for me, but I want to go and see the Bensons on my own, well just with John."

I had to come straight out with it, it was the only way I could do it.

His face showed what he felt and that really got to me. "Why?" was all he said.

"I owe you an explanation I know."

"I think you could say that," he replied.

"The problem is Mike, well it's Sean, the way you feel about him and Jake it's still too raw mate. When you are face to face with them, I think you would lose it, which I'm sure you agree is not what we need at the moment. We need them on edge, not knowing how much we know. You said yourself how hard it is to get anything on them but we have an edge now and that gives us a slim chance. I promise you this Mike, if, I mean when, we get them you will be there to tell them what it's all about. You know what I mean?"

Another one of those pauses. "OK boss, I do understand, If I'm honest with myself I think you're right, I might lose it and we don't need that just now, do we?"

"Thanks Mike." There wasn't much else I could say, he knew how I felt and also knew I was right.

"One thing that I insist on though, Dave. When we've got them – and we will – I get to gloat, face to face. I've got a picture of Sean and Jake here and I want to shove it where he won't ever forget it."

His attitude made me feel a whole lot better and we both visibly relaxed.

"I tell you one thing, Dave," said Mike thoughtfully. "We are getting wound up about these murders because we've seen them or they affect us, but the whole reason this business got started, was because a total stranger picked you, for want of a better description, to look out for her daughter."

"Fuck, you're bloody right, you already said they were looking for her. I bet they are shitting themselves trying to find her."

Mike cut in, "I bet it won't be a happy sibling reunion, all they will want to do is reunite her with Mum, you can bet on that."

"You're so right Mike," I said, "but it can also be a weakness, it makes them, well, desperate. If they are willing to kill, and we know they are, surely it can't be just the money. I mean we are talking bloody mega money here, more than a dozen people could spend in a lifetime, even trying hard."

"Well boss I've been researching all this with our city contacts and it's getting interesting.

Right, Sarah and Lord Benson senior marry around 1988 and, surprise surprise, it appears that it was the real thing, from everything I've been told or read, it was real love.

In the fullness of time, two or three years, Sarah becomes pregnant.

And then something happens which destroys the wedded bliss. What, we don't know, can't even guess seeing as we weren't around at the time.

We can however surmise that it must have been pretty major, because it blew the marriage apart.

Sarah then does a disappearing act, all alone, pregnant, without funds – at least I think we can assume that she would have grabbed anything that she could convert into cash, just to get her started. She would know not to use cards of any sort, because they would trace her in minutes.

"In fact what she did was spot a family who was purchasing a ticket for cash, offered them a large discount to let her pay with a card, when it was all confirmed they gave her the agreed cash.

Now it was a family of five travelling to Italy, which had a double benefit for our girl in as much as she not only got the cash but when the hounds set off looking for her, they followed the card, swarmed all over Italy, convinced our girl was there. This gave her the time she needed to disappear, and it worked like a dream because the bloodhounds never found her, until now anyway.

"Very shrewd our girl considering she was just a kid, but now we have another kid out there, who doesn't know what has happened to her mum and probably not a clue of the danger that she's in herself."

Mike slumped back in his chair for a rest, he doesn't usually talk this much, but I think that the fate of the girl and the evil that was heading her way had got to him.

"With the information that I've been able to glean, this is what I think happened. When Lord B senior sits down to write his will, at a later date, he's still not been able to find them. By this time he's eaten up with guilt and depression at what has happened. I know this is a lot of guesswork, informed guesswork but still guesswork, hopefully one day we might find out the full truth, but until then this is all we've got.

"We keep thinking mostly of the shares but that is only part of it, there are probably six or seven large houses worldwide, plus millions in cash, art, antiques and all the other stuff the wealthy have round them apart from the shares.

So this is how I think the will probably went, and I bet I'm not far out.

"Nigel gets say thirty-five per cent of the shares, the other two get five per cent each. Now Lord B was probably of the opinion that Sarah would bring the child up a lot better than he had his, and had convinced himself that what he was doing was right.

Sarah gets thirty-five per cent and her child twenty per cent. Now that Sarah has been murdered, assuming Mum has left a will, her daughter gets fifty-five per cent and overall control."He paused to allow me to digest the figures.

"It doesn't end there. All the information I've been getting says that Nigel has been preparing to float the company on the stock market; now we are talking billions and billions. Say he sells forty per cent of the company, he keeps control and has enough money to make him one of the most powerful industrialists in the world. That's the stakes we are talking about. Assuming that Nigel knew nothing of the will, which seems pretty certain, can you imagine, he must have gone apoplectic when he realised the ramifications of what was written. I bet he would have wiped out a small country just to appease his anger. How little the three that we know about would have meant."

He slumped back exhausted, it had been a major effort on

Mike's part, not just the speech but the research. We both sat absorbing the facts.

At last I spoke. "Well Mike," I started, "we have got to nail this bastard and you know why?"

"I surely do mate," said Mike,

"because if we don't he is going to wipe us out and I mean all of us. When you said desperate you were right, he seems to have lost the plot and there's no telling what he might do next."

"I'll tell you one thing Mike,' I said, "I'll have to watch myself today." Because now it really was into the lion's den, or what we call Surrey.

CHAPTER FIVE
(SURREY – THE LION'S DEN)

We approached two of the most enormous wrought iron gates I've ever seen. They stood about six metres high, were a mass of scrolls, lions, unicorns, all painted gold or maybe gold leaf with some sort of crest in the centre, the whole thing topped off with some sort of heraldic eagle whose spread-eagled wings covered virtually both gates.

From our vantage point in the car, it made the gates look like one structure, but of course there must be some sort of join to enable the gates to open.

"I think that tells you something about the owner," said John in his laconic, seen-it-all-before style.

But it did hit the nail on the head; I was expecting a big-time megalomaniac.

The gates started to swing open, so we were being observed on camera and they knew exactly who we were. We drove on through and down a long tree-lined drive that stretched out in front of us. It was difficult not to be impressed, it was a bit like having a county as your garden.

I couldn't help but realise that these country houses from the early 1800s and even earlier had a sole purpose which was to intimidate. It sent out a message – I'm top dog! Enter here and you start beneath me. I could see how this could work, I was feeling slightly intimidated. The sheer grandeur and opulence made you feel, I suppose, intimidated was the right word.

After about some eight minutes we crested the brow of a hill and got our first view of the house.

It nestled in a valley about half a mile away. The road curved round gently, eventually arriving at an enormous carriage circle with an extremely large fountain in the centre, which came as no surprise – we were expecting ostentation by this time.

Either side of the road from the crest of the hill where we sat, the trees had been cleared to leave fields of about twenty acres. I suppose to frame the house, which it did perfectly.

But what really struck me was, the two massive fields either side of the road had been mowed; I mean they looked like a bloody bowling green, now that was ostentation, but it worked! The view that was before us was truly magnificent, the whole vista crowned by a truly spectacular house. I must admit to wondering if man would ever build anything to equal this, it was truly beautiful.

We drove on in silence, probably having similar thoughts. We were greeted by two surly looking thugs, for want of a more apt description. What I mean is you were left without any doubt as to what they were there for, it wasn't artistic or intellectual pursuits that was for sure. They showed us into a superb room which I assumed to be the library, the wall-to-wall books gave it away somewhat.

"We will have to search you," said thug number one.

"OK," said John and stepped forward, taking off his coat and handing it to number one who duly patted the coat all round and tossed it onto a chair.

"Do you mind?" said John, grabbing the coat from the chair. Number two took a step forward at this, not anticipating but hoping for an excuse for violence. I stepped forward volunteering myself for searching. I saw John fold his coat and lay it carefully over the chair then offer himself for patting down.

Number two finished my search and we were told to sit down.

"His lordship will be with you in a while, gentlemen," said number one. He was obviously boss thug. They withdrew and stood either side of the door awaiting the second coming. We didn't have to wait long when the door swung open being held by thug number three, and in walked Nigel.

"Hollins," he said.

"Benson," I answered, standing expecting to shake hands. "Lord Benson," he snapped, obviously angry, already showing a weak spot.

"Well that's yet to be established," I replied. "And also it's Mr Hollins."

He looked down, needing some time to control his anger, not a man that is used to having to worry about his outburst or having to consider anybody's feelings. I could see him struggling. "Fair comment, Mr Hollins, I apologise." He was in control again.

"Thank you very much, sir," I answered, holding out my hand to shake his. I still couldn't manage 'your lordship' but he seemed to accept that and shook my hand.

First round to me, I thought.

We sat down opposite each other across his large antique desk. This seemed to settle him and he visibly relaxed.

"I don't think we need the entourage, do we?"

"Fine by me," I replied. I took a good look at him for the first time. He was in his forties, fairly tall with a deep tan, quite good looking with a very easy manner, confident, which I suppose comes with wealth and power, but no sign of the megalomaniac I was expecting. I was a bit surprised.

"Gentlemen, if you wouldn't mind leaving us to our discussions, I'll call you when we've finished."

The thugs leapt to their feet, John looked towards me, I gave him a nod, he stood and walked to the door following the thugs. As the door closed, he spoke.

"Would you like a drink, Mr Hollins?" he said with just a touch of sarcasm.

"No thank you sir, I'm fine thanks."

He poured himself a large drink and sat down.

"What can I do for you? I understand you know my stepmother, is that right? How is she?"

I looked at him long and hard and then replied, "I think the first thing to establish is what I know. Yes, I have got a lot of information from Lady Sarah which we will get to later. Next, as you well know, she is dead, murdered on your orders, please don't waste my time denying it, I'm not the police, I'm of no danger to you. If that's what I wanted I would have gone straight to them with what I know."

He made to reply.

"Please sir, let me finish, then you can say whatever you want."

He gestured that he acquiesced, so I continued. "I can if you so wish tell you the vehicle that was used, in fact I will, it was a Park Ward Continental, early sixties, colour Regal Red. I can tell you not only the registration number but the name of the driver as well, also it's not his first murder for you."

His face was showing the tension he was feeling, a few twitches, a bit of sweat on his upper lip, his whole body language showed it, however much he tried to hide it.

"You can of course prove none of this," he said through gritted teeth while trying to sound confident.

"Don't be ridiculous," I continued. "There would be forensics all over the Bentley, and do you really think Thompson will protect you once it dawns on him that he's going down for murder? You're a lot more trusting than I would be if that's the case."

He looked at me long and hard, took his time and then said, "If what you say is true, surely my best action would be to kill you now, after all you are alone except for the elderly gentleman. I think we can dismiss him."

"Well," I said. 'Number one, please don't take me for stupid, I'm not going to come to your stronghold unprepared, just remember I am a newspaperman, so please believe me when I say I have left a full dossier of everything I know about you and also, believe me, some of it is sensational.

"My team, of course, have full instructions what to do should we not return. Firstly, information will leak to the papers, bearing in mind these are my friends, this coupled with the rumours they will spread means that your business would start to fail within days. By now, the public fuelled by the press will be clambering for your blood.

"Enter the police, armed with my dossier, you will be arrested, they will lean on your henchmen and turn your life inside out. Sooner or later they will start to give you up. You will definitely get life. Probably with a recommendation for a minimum thirty years I would think. I know this is a bit simplistic but I'm sure you realise that whatever the timescale will be, the end result is inevitable. I feel I must, out of courtesy, warn you that the elderly gentleman, should there be trouble, would certainly severely hurt at least three of your thugs which just leaves me one, perhaps the one with the hormone problem, discounting you of course."Shall I continue or are you not interested now you're going to kill us?"

"Please continue."

So off I went again. "If you doubt that I spoke to Sarah let me give you a few facts she gave me. Firstly, her pet name for your father was Nap. She used to kid him that he was like Napoleon and had dreams of ruling Europe, right? This place, thirty-six rooms, ten bathrooms, stabling for fourteen horses, the other stables are converted into garages. They married in Guildford register office, spent their honeymoon on Kalymnos, a small

Greek island off the Turkish coast, shall I go on or do you believe me now?""I believe you have spoken with her."

"I'll continue then. Your father Gordon made a will, unbeknown to you he left substantial shares in the company to Sarah and her child, you have now had Sarah killed, who herself left a will, leaving everything to her daughter. Yes, she had a daughter, you didn't know that did you, when you jumped the gun and killed Sarah? How did you know by the way that she was back? I bet she rang you hoping to sort out your problems. You thought you had solved all the problems by killing her, but all you did was give her daughter, your half-sister, a controlling share in the company. She is, by the way, eighteen and therefore old enough to take control."

Nigel was pale. I must have been pretty close to the truth. It seemed that he hadn't known of the daughter, although his father had mentioned a child in the will, or so we thought, he had not been able to trace her and had assumed she did not exist.

"I think our business is concluded, don't you?"

"If you say so," I replied, wondering if we would get out alive. As if by magic, the thugs appeared. I supposed there was some kind of button to summon them. They were closely followed by John.

"Our guests are leaving now," said Nigel.

I could see he was still undecided whether to take the chance and kill us or not.

"Just one more thing before we go.""I don't know what came over me but I was extremely angry and really felt like stirring things up, looking back a really dangerous thing to do.

"Which one of you is Gary Thompson?" I looked along

the line. All three were looking doubtful and unsure of what to do next, they were all thuggish looking as I said one and two were about six foot two inches the third about six foot seven with a build to match.

"I am," came more of a grunt really.

"I just wanted to see what you looked like," I said, "because I have a good friend who's longing to meet you, because you killed his best friend and little boy just five years old."

"Why you ..." Another grunt, and he surged at me, pulling a gun as he came.

I didn't quite see what happened then, but Gary sunk to his knees choking and gasping, making all sorts of terrible noises. His gun was gently plucked from his fingers, the cartridge clip ejected and the gun thrown onto the desk in front of Nigel, all with one hand by John. I was now watching the proceedings with a degree of pleasure; watching a master is always enjoyable.

He must have hit Gary in the throat somewhere, all too fast for us to follow even though we knew something had happened. It was certainly devastating to Gary who was still gasping horribly on his knees.

This all happened in a split second, but thug number one was beginning to move on John. I was about to shout but there was no need. John had tackled Gary purposely with one hand so as to leave the other hand free should he need it, which he now did.

As number one moved in, John's hand went up to the back of his neck just behind his ears and he took a grip, which stopped him in his tracks, his arms drooped and he sort of hung like he was paralysed. He was still conscious, at least I think he was.

The other two were now also beginning to move. John dropped number one on the floor now unconscious and a gun appeared in his hand pointing straight at them. They stopped. They had seen what the elderly gentleman was capable of and were not keen to tackle him, especially when he was pointing a gun at them.

Everybody stood still, number one out on the floor, Gary still on his knees choking.

"I did warn you," I said to Nigel.

"I think you had better go now, right now," he snapped.

I stood and we backed towards the door, John shielding me just in case they got their courage back.

"By the way," said John,

"he will wake up soon." He pointed to number one.

"And he'll be OK. That one will need a bit of treatment." He pointed to Gary Thompson. "He has a damaged voice box, it won't kill him but he won't be able to talk for a few days."

We exited and made for the main door, keeping an eye on the library door just in case they came charging through it shooting, but no one appeared. We got in the car and left as quick as we could. As we approached the gates they were still closed.

"Would this break through them?" I asked.

"Not a chance! It may be a Range Rover but you would need a tank to break through them."

As we drew closer to the entrance, the gates began to open, so Nigel had decided, now was not the time to kill us! We had surprised him this time, but he would not underestimate next time. We would need to take extreme care from now on.

"Where did you learn all that?" I asked

"All what?" he replied.

"All that paralysing people, emptying guns with one hand, all too fast for the human eye?" I must admit to smiling at this stage. "And producing a gun when you had been searched", a fact that had slipped my mind until now.

"Well," he said pensively, "the grips and things I've learnt at various places round the world on many little jobs that I've been involved in, also when faced with more than one opponent having one hand free is standard procedure and as it turned out very wise. The gun was easy. I gave them my coat to search first, when they had finished and threw it on the chair I made a big deal of folding it carefully myself, taking the opportunity to transfer my gun to the coat, then they searched me, all clear! Which left me to retrieve my coat and transfer the gun back to my pocket at my leisure. All of these things you would have spotted when you were working with me. Which proves you've been a newspaperman too long."

I felt a slight rebuke which I could not argue with.

"Also, of course, these types, well people in general, dismiss the older person, but concentrate on watching you closely. This gives me a big advantage which I enjoy immensely." I couldn't help thinking that he didn't need much in the way of help from any source. But in view of my conversation with Nigel earlier, his insight was quite breathtaking. I must admit to wondering just how dangerous he could be and how pleased I was that he was on my team.

You do realise that Gary's position is very dodgy now that you've named him and his crime, also the Bentley. He must dispose of that now if he has any sense at all."

"I agree," I replied.

"I must plead guilty to losing it and surrendering to an overwhelming desire to stir things up somewhat. I just wanted to let him know that he's not safe and untouchable, that we can get to him. Not a wise move in hindsight, but I did get a bit carried away, oh well!"

"One thing's for sure," said John, "he will be extremely

41

dangerous now. I think it would be wise if I looked after Caroline for a while and I'll get a couple of mates to watch the door at the office. What do you think?""Absolutely! You're right, but remember, John, he won't underestimate you again, they will want you as much as Caz. You humiliated them today and they won't forgive that in a hurry."

Having said that, there was nobody I would trust more to look after my wife or anyone near and dear than John, and no one who could do it better, I was certain of that.

We drove in silence for some time, both wondering what we had unleashed and where it was going to end, both knowing that we couldn't back out now, but would keep going until the end, however it turned out.

"What did you mean when you said that you had warned him?" asked John.

"I told him you would leave one to me and severely hurt the others." He nodded.

We drove on in silence.

CHAPTER SIX (IT STARTS)

We pulled into the office car park, locked the Range Rover and entered the building. We were greeted by Mike looking distraught.

"What's wrong Mike?"

I must admit I was worried that it had begun and we had been caught cold.

"Well boss, it's a bloody nightmare."

"Christ Mike, what is it?" I wanted to grab him and shake him.

Mike took a deep breath and spoke. "It's the bank, I don't know why but they've stopped all payments on everything, the quarterly lease, cheques returned and the phone has been going mad. I don't know what to tell them, it just doesn't make any sense."

"Yes it does Mike, I'll explain later." But I knew it had begun, just not in the way I'd expected but it had begun all right. Now we had to fight back.

"Right Mike, I want the CEO of our bank, I think it's Sir Michael Perry, don't take no for an answer, then I want our branch manager, Stanley Marr, but first I want Charmicheals, Jimmy if possible."

Charmicheals was the company solicitors, Jimmy was the son and an old friend that I had nicknamed 'the Pit Bull'. Given a task to do, he would go at it viciously until he got what he wanted. He had been an invaluable ally on many occasions, perhaps again now when we really need him.

"Firstly though John, you get to Caz. And sort your mates for here, OK?"

"Consider it done, sir." He was right into military mode now, which made me feel good that everything would be done. With that he was gone.

Mike entered the office. "Jimmy Charmicheal on line one." "Forget the other calls till I tell you, Mike.""Right boss," he answered.

"Jimmy," I greeted him warmly, "I'm having a few problems with my bank and I thought I'd better talk to you before I talk to their COE."I went on to fill him in on what had happened. I omitted the full story, just the banking part.

"They can't bloody do that!" he shouted. "At least as long as you're solvent. You are solvent, I take it?"

"Yes of course I am, we have a contingency account with two million in it, our current account has about £500,000, it varies between a million and zero. We also have a permanent overdraft facility of a million, which we have never used as yet."

"Bloody Nora, you're richer than me, you bugger, I must be in the wrong business."

I did then go on to tell him that I thought there had been pressure bought to bear by Lord Benson and his companies.

"You are upsetting some big boys, aren't you? Old boy, PLEASE, PLEASE, let me sue them. I'll take them for a fortune, restriction of trade libel, insider trading, no lights on his bike! It's never ending, I'm going to have such fun.""Wait just a minute Jimmy, before you start biting anybody's leg, here's what I would like you to do. Phone Sir Michael Perry their CEO. Tell him that I'm suing and could you have his solicitor's details so you can forward the relevant paperwork direct to them. When you've done that, ring me and tell me what he said, straight away if you could mate."

He rang back within a matter of minutes.

"By god, I enjoyed that old boy. He had a motion I'm

sure while I was still threatening him with everything short of deportation. Anyway the gist was, to leave it with him and he would sort it. God that was fun, PLEASE sue, just for me."I always enjoy talking to Jimmy; he enjoys his job so much, and there's nobody better that's for sure. So for now I think a cup of tea and wait. So I thank him and say I would get back to him.

I didn't have to wait long before Mike entered the office. "Sir Michael Perry for you."

I waited for as long as I thought appropriate and then answered. "Sir Michael, this is a surprise, what can I do for you?" I gestured for Mike to sit down.

"I've just had your solicitor on the phone talking about suing the bank, I just thought if we spoke man to man we could sort this matter out."

I paused for a few seconds to let him wonder, then I answered.

"The thing is, Sir Michael, I'll be perfectly frank with you, the bank, your bank has shat on us disgracefully. I know that pressure is being applied on yourselves by Lord Benson, please don't deny it." It was a statement not a question. "Now I find it hard to believe that you would attack the media by choice, especially when you are so blatantly in the wrong as I'm certain you are aware. You must know the damage that we could do to your reputation, should we choose.

"You have spoken to my solicitor and I'm sure you know of his reputation, which, I can assure you is well deserved."

"I'm admitting nothing. I'm hoping this can be off the record," he said quietly.

"But something is on your mind I can tell, so let's have it."

"Well, I have no desire to sue you, I am well aware who my enemy is and will be dealing with that matter in due course, but I must have my banking facilities back to normal!"

"So what do you suggest?" he asked.

I could tell by his whole manner he was embarrassed by the situation and wanted out. He was by reputation an honest man, which showed the pressure his lordship could bring to bear.

"This is what I suggest. I'll contact Stanley Marr, our branch manager, and persuade him to stop all this nonsense. I think I can persuade him, but should there be a problem, I'll tell him to contact you. It would be better that it was sorted in branch then no blame can be laid at your door by you-know-who. I take it there was never direct contact with you so he would find it difficult to make waves?"

"I won't ask how you will persuade him, but without doubt I'm sure you will. Perhaps when this is all over we can meet, perhaps have lunch, under better circumstances."

"I'd like that very much," I answered.

"There is one more thing, the shares in a certain person's businesses, I would strongly advise selling because I feel that they are going to fall substantially very soon."

He coughed and then said, "I'm not sure how legal this is, but I will take note and act accordingly. Thank you and good luck in your mission, he is a formidable enemy as I'm sure you realise. I really hope to meet you soon."

With that he was gone.

Mike was looking somewhat bemused, a smile spread across his face.

"I tell you one thing, Mike," I said.

"I met the driver that you want to meet, I told him that you were anxious to meet him and would be catching up with him later."

The colour drained from his face. I knew then I was right not to take him, he would have lost it and definitely have tried to kill him there and then; he would have no chance to control himself and he knew it.

"What did he say?"

"He went for me with a gun, but fortunately John did something particularly nasty to him which left him gasping and choking, he looked like he was fighting for life to be honest. John says a few days in hospital should see him all right though."

"Shame," was all Mike said.

I never told him that John thought Gary's days were numbered because of my loose comments about Sean and Jake's murders, but we will just have to wait and see.

"Right, now for Mr Marr."

While I called the bank I told Mike about the extra security that John was arranging.

"Things could get very nasty any time now, as I'm sure you realise." He just nodded.

I heard a voice on the phone.

"Hello, could I speak to Mr Marr? It's David Hollins, tell him that I insist on speaking to him. Do not come back and tell me he's in a meeting or any excuse, because I can be there in a few minutes and he will be very sorry should that happen."

She went quiet and must have passed on my message because the next voice I heard was his.

"M-Mr Hollins, er what can I do for you?"

"I want you to listen to me carefully Mr Marr. When you fucked with my bank account, you obviously didn't take into consideration that you were dealing with a press agency. We are truly the world's nosiest of people therefore you should have considered this could be a problem for you."

"What do you mean, Mr Hollins?" he said nervously.

"Well," I continued, beginning to enjoy myself, "here's the thing, being so nosey we like to keep a dossier on everybody we have dealings with, just to give us an insight into their character should we ever need it. Do you understand Mr Marr?" I paused.

"I understand what you're saying, but I can't see how it would affect me."

"I'll be honest," I continued, "I'm looking at your file as we speak, there are some pictures of you and a young lady, who incidentally looks somewhat familiar. Anyway, being as delicate as I can, it looks like you are giving her or perhaps she is giving you some sort of performance-related bonus that we keep reading about in the press." I waited.

"I do not see that my relationship with Miss Gordon has anything to do with you or our business dealings."

He was blustering and he knew it.

"I have no interest whatsoever Mr Marr, but I think perhaps her father, boyfriend or even your very own wife would be very interested, what do you think?"

"What do you want?" He knew he was beaten and had accepted there was a price to pay.

"My accounts back to normal within the hour, you can phone any involved parties and explain that it was entirely the bank's mistake. You can also inform Mr Thompson that I have a file on him, which is even more interesting than yours.

I have already spoken to Sir Michael who wants this business finished with, you can of course verify this." If you're brave enough, I thought.

Mr Thompson was his area boss and probably gave the orders in the first place.

"OK Mr Hollins, leave it to me. I hope I can rely on your discretion over the other matter!"

"My lips are sealed Mr Marr, absolutely. Just one piece of advice though, never choose to make enemies of the press because they have knowledge, and it's always difficult to win against someone who has knowledge."

"Yes I can see that, no hard feelings I hope."

"None whatsoever, I know you had outside pressure and I know where from, but I can assure you there are no hard feelings." And I meant it, he was just doing what he was told after all. I put the phone down.

Mike pensively said, "I didn't know we had files on everybody?"

"We don't but perhaps we should from now on," I replied.

At least we could still laugh, and we did.

"By the way Mike, do you know a Miss Gordon at the bank?? "Yes," he replied.

"Nice looking, early twenties, blonde, quite shy, seems a nice girl."

"Mm, obviously not as shy as you thought." I decided to leave it at that.

CHAPTER SEVEN (PLANS)

I felt we needed to get everyone together, the staff, and let them know what was going on. They would already know something was afoot, but until they were told it was just rumour. I got Mike to get them together in my office, it was a squeeze but would suit our purpose. There was myself and Mike, June Wright, David Kirby, Roger Delore and Mary Jones, six in all seven including John, who was with Caz. This then was our merry band, most had been with me since I first started. They were the best in their field, we turned round more work than other agencies with four times our staff, so you can understand when I say these people were not staff but more like family and I would do anything to protect them.

"Right gang, we have a small problem!" It gained their attention. "Mike and I are working on something which could – and I stress could – put us all in a bit of danger. So John is getting a couple of his hoods to guard the door to stop any undesirables getting in and of course to protect you. If you notice anything unusual or if you think you are being followed watched or anything, and I stress anything, don't take chances, go to Mike, John, or one of his men and listen to what they say. Also make sure you lock up at night."

"Is it anything to do with Benson?" asked June. I suppose it was a bit naïve to employ the best bloodhounds in the business and then expect them not to sniff out the slightest bit of information. How they do it I've no idea but I shouldn't be surprised after all this time.

"I think it's best that you don't know any details as yet.

You will obviously know everything eventually but until then it's safer for you not to know."

They nodded their agreement, but I knew they would be digging around finding out what they could.

"I will be going away for a few days, Mike will be in charge, any problems go to him, any security problems he can always contact John. Remember, if you are worried about anything, and I mean anything, don't keep quiet, see Mike and he'll get it sorted. These people we are dealing with are not nice and I do not want anybody hurt because of what I'm doing, OK?"

Another nod.

"How long will you be away?" This time it was Mary.

"I'm not sure as yet, but I'm hoping it won't be more than a few days."

They accepted what I had said and were each digesting it in their own way.

"OK then, Mike will keep you up to speed and let's hope it all gets sorted asap."

That signalled to everybody that the meeting was over, and they went back to whatever they were doing and left me to my thoughts.

I grabbed Mary as she left. "Mary, could you get your boyfriend on the phone and ask if he and the inspector could come and see me, straight away if possible. Stress that it's urgent."

I think she blushed slightly and mumbled something I couldn't understand. I must stop teasing her! I sat contemplating what was happening. Should I be acting as I was? I was, after all, putting us all in danger, there was no doubt about that. I felt really guilty but what option did I have? To ignore what I knew, to leave Benson to kill whoever he pleased? I knew for sure his next victim would be Lady

Sarah's daughter. Could I possibly sit back and allow that? Then of course there was me, Mike, Caz and anyone his sick mind thought might be a threat. I couldn't ignore that. "Of course you can't, why do you think I chose you?"

"Oh my god she's back." I knew straight away it was Sarah. "Why did you choose me?"

"I've no idea, perhaps there's a higher power than us involved here."

"Please don't start all that bloody mumbo jumbo, that will finish me off." I couldn't stop myself.

"Let me assure you that I'm as much a sceptic as you when it comes to the supernatural, or I was! I can't really say that now can I? Considering I'm conversing with you from, well I don't really know where from, but certainly not the same place as you. Just explain to me how come I picked without knowing, the one person who not only had the courage, but had the honour not to leave Maggie to her fate. All of this I knew just by looking at you once. Please explain that to me."

I couldn't give her an explanation, because there wasn't one, this was one of those times that you just had to accept what was happening and not waste your time and energy trying to explain it, which you never could. I think, truly I knew this right from when she had grabbed me after the accident.

"I can't," I said, "but I will promise you one thing."

"What's that?" said Sarah.

"I promise that I will do everything I can to look after Maggie."

"I know that, David, I've always known it."

"Mr Hollins, Mr Hollins!"

I could feel myself being shaken.

"Inspector Densil and Dusty will be here within fifteen minutes." It was Mary's voice.

"You fell asleep, I came to tell you and had to wake you up."

"Thanks Mary." I was fully awake now.

"Just show them in when they arrive, and thanks."

She left and inevitably I started to wonder, was it all a dream? Did I just talk to a dead person? The only thing I knew for certain, that no matter what, there was no turning back, we were in it to the end, any other outcome, other than winning was unacceptable, In fact I must admit it made me shudder just to contemplate any alternative. I had opened the door to all sorts of evil and had no choices.

The door opened and Mary showed in Inspector Densil and Sergeant Millar.

"Come in gentlemen, please sit yourselves down."

They settled themselves down and looked towards me in obvious anticipation.

"What can we do for you sir?" asked the inspector.

I took a good look at the inspector. He was in his forties, six foot plus, heavy build and always calm and quiet but not a man you would want to upset, all in all, a man I warmed to as soon as I met him. I don't think I will change my mind. Sergeant Millar, on the other hand, was like a terrier jumping at everything, a likeable lad and with the inspector's mentoring would become a very good detective.

"Well Inspector, it's more what I can do for you."

"Oh yes, and what's that then?"

"I think it would be best if I tell you what I know in one go, save all the stop-and-start banter."

He nodded his agreement, and I carried on.

"The first thing is the identity of the hit-and-run victim." I could see their interest pick up straight away. "The woman was Lady Sarah Benson."

At this the sergeant really wanted to jump in, but was

restrained by the inspector raising an arm. They were really hooked now, I wondered how much they already knew. Not too much judging by their obvious interest, so I continued.

"She was killed by a man called Gary Thompson, around forty, fair hair, scar on his right cheek, at present in hospital, I should think the Royal Surrey. The car was a Bentley Park Ward continental early sixties, I've written all the details including the colour and registration number, and a full description of Thompson." I passed the paper I'd been holding to the inspector.

"Thanks," he said. "Just a few questions though, where did you get all this information from and why didn't you tell us all this the other day, when we first spoke to you?""I can't let you know my sources, you know that. I've given you the facts, now I'm sure you can find the evidence once your forensic boys get to that vehicle. I never had the full information when we spoke previously.""That's fair enough, but one word of caution, I assume that the person behind all this is Lord Nigel Benson, son of Lord Gordon Benson of Langham Park, Surrey.""I didn't know it was called that when we called on him, but you've got the right family."

He looked at me as though I was insane. "You called on him?"

"I certainly did," I answered, "and it was quite interesting, I can assure you."

"You obviously know how dangerous he is," he said, "so what happened, David?"I gave him a pretty full rundown of our visit. I'd noticed he called me David and guessed we were allies now, which pleased me no end. When I got to the part concerning John, he interrupted. "Would this be John Penn?"

"Yes," I answered, "do you know him?"

"Only by reputation and he has some reputation in

security circles."

"I've served with him many times, and the reputation comes nowhere near the reality, believe me," I said.

"Even so, you were lucky to get out at all, believe me," said the inspector.

"I realise that. I think he was unsure of how much we knew and that made him hold back a bit. I do think a storm is coming though, and we are taking as many precautions as is possible."

"Well," said the inspector, "you seem to know what you are doing, you'll need to with that lot."

"It sounds like you have some previous with the Bensons, is that right?" I said, following an overwhelming feeling that we had touched a nerve and he wanted to share something which to him was important.

He gave me a look as if assessing how far I could be trusted. I think he decided that we were on the same side and had a better chance joining forces.

He paused.

"That scrote Gary Thompson, we've met before. I was then in Special Branch, just made sergeant, my inspector was a Bill Meeks, nice bloke, and a good honest copper. We had been called to a killing because it involved a bomb. Somebody had blown up a little terraced house, killing an Indian family, Mum, Dad and three kids. We looked into it, it was obviously not a terrorist incident.

"What our investigations told us was it was the last property in the street that refused to sell, thus holding up a major development being built on the old dock site by, guess who? Yes, Benson Construction and Development Co.

"They had offered Mr Ghannur, the Indian family that owned the house, a substantial amount to move, but he would only go if they found him a house in a certain road. This was proving difficult, hence the delay.

"We strongly suspected the Bensons who were virtually untouchable in those days, but we went to question them anyway.

"During the meeting – his lordship wasn't available by the way – we met his development director and a Mr Gary Thompson! "Anyway, we had to hear all the platitudes, condolences to the relatives, a terrible tragedy, etc. You know the form.

We had just got up to leave when the lovely Gary in his wisdom pipes up. 'We offered bloody Ghunga Din good money to go, he wouldn't, and now we'll get it for bugger all, stupid sod'.

"Bill Meeks turned round, picked up the phone from the desk, one of those big square things that we had in those days, and smashed it straight into Thompson's face with tremendous force.

"He said, 'You fucking bastard.' Thompson had gone out like a light, claret everywhere. I swear that if I hadn't been there, he would have killed him. He already had his arm raised for the follow-up blow when I grabbed him. He took some stopping, I can assure you. Anyway, when we left, Thompson was being taken to hospital with the side of his face hanging open and threats of every law suit imaginable, screaming from his companion's mouth.

"Once I got him quietened down, I started to ease the story from him. It turned out that his old dad had lived next door to the Ghannurs, they had looked after him all the time he was ill, right up till he died. Bill had grown very close to them over the years he had known them. He was still in a state of shock but he didn't try to hide how he felt. 'They were diamonds, salt of the earth, they treated my dad like one of the family. I just couldn't have scum like that abusing that lovely family. You know as well as I do they killed them, just to save a few pounds. I should have finished that little shit.'

"'BILL,' I shouted at him, knowing I had to get through to him somehow. 'Listen, It's you we've got to get sorted out not them! This could finish you if not worse.' He nodded.

"All hell did break loose as you can imagine. I think it was the fear of publicity, which we did make veiled threats about, leaving him in no doubt that we would make sure he got the maximum. Which in the end persuaded Lord B. to drop it.

"Unfortunately, it didn't help Bill. He had no option but to resign, he only kept his pension because I made it plain to the men in suits that I would stand up in court and swear that Thompson had attacked him and they realised that I meant it, so they didn't push it too much.

"Shortly afterwards I was transferred out of Special Branch into CID. And inspector is as high as I'll ever go, and that's the previous you asked about."

I could see the emotion and anger telling me had awakened and I felt for him.

"Bloody hell, these people have made some enemies!" I couldn't help but observe.

"So what happened to Bill Meeks?"

"Oh he does a bit of security work when he can get it. I guide people to him when I can, but Benson's put the word out which makes it difficult. A great shame, he was one of the best investigators I ever met."

"I'll tell you what Inspector, if he's as good as you say we can certainly use him, a good investigator is gold dust to us. Finding someone you can trust and is discrete is our problem." I passed him a card.

"Here's John's number, get him to ring and you can tell him we are after his old friends, that should please him."

"You won't regret it David, I'd stake my life on that."
"I'm sure of that Inspector.' His recommendation was all I
needed. The feelings of respect and warmth for the inspector
were growing the more

I got to know him. The thought came to me that his
lordship must be underestimating the quality of the force
that was growing against him.

I could only hope that his megalomania was such that
he dismissed everyone as inferior and therefore not a threat.

I must admit a definite feeling of confidence was beginning
to grow.

I must guard against being confident, the people we were
up against are rich, powerful and ruthless, but we were a
formidable group, plus of course we had help from the other
side.

"We must get going, Sergeant. We need to get down to
Surrey, have a word with the lord and grab his Bentley. Get
onto the forensic boys and tell them to be ready for our call."

"Right boss." He was already dialling.

The inspector stood up, leaned over the desk and held out
his hand to shake mine. I knew now that we were part of the
same team, and that suited me; these two were a fine team.

"I suppose I'll have to wait until you are ready before you
tell me the whole story," said the inspector, giving me a look
to let me know that he knew there was more that I wasn't
telling.

"I'll be away for a few days, Inspector, but just talk to Mike
if there's anything you need, or you need to get a message to
me, and by the way, I'll tell you everything when I can."

"OK David," he said. "And by the way, it's Charlie,
right?" They stood up and said their goodbyes and left.

"Good luck," I called after them. "And you mate," came
the reply.

CHAPTER EIGHT (MAGGIE)

Once they left, I started to formulate my next moves, which would involve the third share I had with two mates in a light aircraft, a Cessna 340A to be precise. It was, I suppose, a boy's toy, but to us three it was a passion and my one indulgence, and very practical at times, well that's what I tell myself. We shared it on a rota basis. Although it was not my time, I was hoping that Jay and Carl would allow me; usually we helped each if at all possible. We had been friends since school and remained good friends still.

I spoke to them both starting with Carl. They both agreed straight away, for the price of a good meal out including their wives. I was happy to agree, seeing that I had been best man at both their weddings and loved them both, including the wives, like sisters I hasten to add.

Once I'd secured the plane, I called Jay back. He answered and was somewhat surprised to hear it was me again.

"What's going on mate?" he asked.

Now Jay was a bit of a pirate! So I thought he would be a bit more amenable to what I had planned than Carl, who, being an accountant and living up to the popular image we all have of accountants, liked everything to be proper. He won't be pleased when he reads that, but it's the truth! Sorry mate.

"Well Jay, I would like you to file a flight plan for tomorrow, with you as the pilot, flying to Italy, with a course that takes me across Spain."

There was one of those pauses again while Jay tried to decide what on earth I could be up to.

"It's nothing nasty, is it?"

"You have my word, and I will make sure there is no comeback on you."

"I know that mate, I'm just worrying what you might be getting yourself into, but you know I'll do

it, in fact I'll get on it right now. You're sure you aren't getting in over your head, aren't you?"I felt guilty not being able to tell him, but the fewer people that knew what was going on the better. "Listen mate, when we go for our meal I'll tell you all about it."

He wouldn't believe it if I told him anyway. He would have already sussed that Spain was my real destination but wouldn't ask any more questions.

I called Mike into the office and told him I was flying out to get Maggie and explained about the flight plan.

"So I take it you're going to land in Spain because that is where she is, right?""Right."

"Won't you be reported missing when you don't arrive in Italy?""Eventually yes, but they will then check the UK, Jay will fog everything as much as possible, they must have mistaken the names, blah blah, but he will have to tell them in the end. All this should give me at least a week, which should be ample." Hopefully I thought.

"I hope you know what you are doing, boss."

"Well I hope so too Mike, but we have to fight these people, we don't have a choice, it's them or us, I'm sure you agree with that!""Absolutely boss, it's been eating at me ever since Sean and Jakie. There were quite a few times when I wanted to get a gun and take revenge myself, I can tell you that. So all this is just what I wanted, at last someone's taking them on."

"Well I'm glad you feel like that and I'm glad you never got that gun."

Mike nodded in agreement. "There is something I've got to tell you actually, we've got a copy of the will, Lord B. senior, and it's more or less what we thought. I've sent a copy to Charmicheals to give it the once over just to make sure. And John's doormen have arrived, they are down in reception."

"Great on both counts," I said. "I'll go and see them in a while, you make sure that everyone does what these guys tell them because if John sent them, they're the best!" I was just so pleased that John was getting some protection in place in case of trouble.

"Right Mike, while I'm away you can contact me by email. I shall only turn my phone on at midday and 9.30 in the evening just for a few seconds in case they are trying to track me. I don't know how good they are but I don't want to take any chances."

"OK boss, I'll keep it to a minimum to be careful, and good luck, I wish I could go with you.""It's better if I can sneak in and out without them noticing me. I would really like to be on my way home before they start to look."

We went through a few work-related issues and Mike left. I had an email to send and didn't want anybody watching, just in case, what they don't know etc.

I was contacting an old friend who lives just outside of Ronda in Andalusia. I needed some help from him, but discreetly; I didn't want to endanger him or his family.

We had known each other since we were kids and stayed friends through all sorts of mishaps. Stan, that's his name, had started an import/export company buying shiploads of goods that nobody wanted and finding someone who did, then selling it on, at a profit of course, without it ever leaving the boat. He did this for years, very successfully living a very affluent lifestyle, when suddenly it fell apart. I never knew why, never really asked, it happened and he moved on. Him and his wife moved to Spain in a motorhome, settling eventually just outside of Ronda.

I think partially to get away from the tax man and creditors, and to gain some peace.

He had always been an expert ornithologist, even written books on the subject and was very well respected in that world by people who know.

So he studied the local wildlife and bird life then started taking tourists on trips through the Serrano De Ronda and surrounding areas, and now travels the world as a wildlife guide to all sorts of beautiful if remote places. He's sort of a David Attenborough with luxury hotels, he doesn't like to rough it! He says he doesn't earn much money but he seems happy. I think he's happy with his lot for the present.

I'd had second thoughts about emailing him, so I shouted for Mike. He put his head round the door

"Yes boss, what's up?"

"Could someone go out and get me a pay-as-you-go phone? It's got to have internet, email and all that shit."

"Here, have mine, I've got pay-as-you-go for my work phone and contract for my personal phone."

"Is that right they can't trace them?"

"Well that's not strictly true, but that one's registered to M. Brando so even if they do trace it, it will do them no good at all."

"Why does nobody tell me anything?" I said a bit embarrassed at my lack of knowledge. Still, I learn fast, I'd have to.

I told Mike to get himself one to replace it just in case I lose or damage it, or even get it taken from me. Who knows what the next few days will bring?

Mike left and I dialled Spain. It rang.

"*Ola*." It was Stan.

"Hello boy, how the devil are you?" Pause.

"Come on me old mate, let's have a few words then."

"Is that you Manus?" which was a nickname he gave me when we were still at school and he's the only one who ever uses it. "And if it is, since when have you been speaking Spanish? And like a bloody local too.""It's a long story, I will tell you some time, but not just yet." I could hardly tell him that I learnt it instantly from a dead woman. Stan doesn't question things a lot but that might just stretch his trust a bit.

I found it a bit strange myself, how I could slip into Spanish without a thought, perfectly naturally as if I'd always spoken it. I pushed on, didn't want to give him time to think. "Listen mate, I've got a bit of a favour I want from your good self." I'd switched to English now and he answered the same. "Just ask away, you know I'll do it if I can."

"The thing is, you have got to be very careful, only do what I ask you and no more, don't get involved and above all don't get noticed, we are dealing with some very heavy blokes."

"Bloody hell, you've got me really interested now. What on earth have you got yourself involved in?"

He's always ribbing me about dodgy stories I get tangled up with. I just tell him it's part of the job, but not this time.

"This time mate, it is heavy, these people have killed and will kill again without giving it a second thought, so if you don't want to get involved that's fine, no worries. I'll be perfectly honest, if I wasn't such an awkward bastard, who's too far in to get out, I'd probably think twice.""What and leave all the fun for you? Not likely old boy, anyway you couldn't get out of anything without my help when we were at school, so what makes you think you can manage without me now?"

I knew he would react just like that, but of course I was still troubled by the people I was putting in serious danger. I couldn't see what other options I had. I just had to hope I got everything right and nobody got hurt. It was not like the military, these were civilians, people I cared about, who didn't have any understanding of the horror that people can unleash on their fellow man.

"Just keep it in mind, OK?""Will do. You know me, I don't like to take risks if I can help it."

I dropped the subject of danger then. I could tell it was beginning to embarrass him somewhat.

"OK mate here we go, you remember taking us to a little restaurant at that village in the mountains, Grazalema, the one with all the orange trees outside, where we sat? It's right next to the church of La Auroro in the Plaza De Espana, Los Naranjos I think."

All this detail was not just because Lady Sarah had briefed me, but we had all spent some good times there on our many visits. It was much more old Spain, not the Costas full of expats and English breakfasts. It was a lovely white mountain village with its own uniquely Spanish smell, the heat, fresh food cooking outside, fresh bread no matter what time of day, there was always that smell I've never experienced anywhere else and of course the livestock with the freedom to roam at will. I think we all have our vision or memory of a place that has left good memories and it stays forever.

"Yes, know it very well, but why Los Narangos?"

"Well working in that restaurant is an English girl called Maggie, about eighteen, tall, striking to look at and blonde."

"Hang on a minute Manus, there is only one blonde girl about eighteen or so, calls herself Magdalena, but she's Spanish, she speaks Spanish like a native, even has an Andalusian accent, I'd swear she was local."

"So do I, do I not?" There was a long pause. "There are some very strange things occurring here my old mate, I think I'll just do what you ask and not dig too deep."

"Think that's best, Jonesie," which was my nickname for him. "Right, I want you to talk to her, discreetly, tell her that her mum's sending me to pick her up, that I'll be there in the next few days, to pack a backpack and wear walking shoes and not to tell a soul, stress that please.

If she seems suspicious, you can say that her mum's maiden name is Conway, her dog, who died last June, was called Pepe, he was bitten by a snake and there was nothing they could do for him.

"PLEASE don't make it noticeable to any prying eyes, and keep your eyes open, make sure you're not being watched or followed, or even if she's being watched."

"I'm bloody filling up here, that poor bloody dog, you know what a sucker I am for dogs."

"You shut up you bloody prick," I snapped. "Just make sure you get it right. If you think you've been spotted, give it up and go home and leave it to me."

"There you go again, and what's this about a mum? You've not been a naughty boy have you? Or is she yours? I seem to remember you being a bit of a dog in your younger days, me old Manus."

"Nothing like that mate," I said quietly. "In fact they've murdered her mum, and she doesn't know as yet, I've got that pleasure to look forward to."

I'd forgotten that the restaurant was one of his regular stops with his tourists, so he would know her well, he would have been in there every few days throughout the season, so his distress was real and personal.

"Do what you can Jonesie and make sure you're bloody careful."

"You leave it with me mate, I'll sort her out for you."I went on to tell him that when this was all over I would fly him and Jenny his wife over for the big dinner. I thought I could tell all of them the truth at one time. I don't think I could repeat it more than once. I gave him the mobile number and said to text if there was a problem. I didn't expect him to need it, he was a born survivor and would handle anything that came along, I hope.

CHAPTER NINE (PRESSURE ON)

There was one more job still to do so I said my goodbyes and hung up. I was still being haunted by the fear that I could be putting people close to me in danger and I didn't like the feeling that I wasn't in control, but I was waiting for events to unfold. Perhaps I had been out of the forces too long as John's always telling me. I don't remember anxiety like this, but I was young then, perhaps it's just that you care more as you get older. Also in the military everything is about control and everyone is trained for the job not just thrust into a situation. The phone rang and snapped me out of thinking too much.

"Hello," I said.

"Dave it's Charlie Densil," came the reply.

"Hi Inspector, what can I do for you?"

"Well I've a bit of news for you, we called on Lord B. as we said we would. He denied all knowledge of everything of course. And listen to this, the Bentley has been crushed, would you believe that?""Why on earth would he do that?"

"He said the gearbox had gone and he couldn't be bothered to spend a few thousand on an old car. He had all the relevant paperwork just waiting to show us, very convenient!"I was a bit shocked to say the least.

"That car is worth at least £80,000, can you imagine someone scrapping that just because the gearbox is playing up? I don't think so.

He was panicked into it because we were getting close.

That's me and my big mouth."

"That's just how we see it," he answered. "You haven't heard the best bit yet, we never got to question Gary

Thompson."

"Why, what happened?" I already had a strange feeling but I had to know.

"Someone got to him before us and killed him. They injected air straight into his cannula, causing an embolism. He died within minutes."

"They must be shitting themselves Charlie, don't you think? This all smacks of panic and that's when they make mistakes hopefully."

"Absolutely, I also reckon he was tipped off we were coming and when I find out by who, they'll be fucking sorry." The inspector obviously thought somebody on this team had tipped them off and he was really pissed off. "I wouldn't like to be in his way that's for sure." Just his voice made the hairs on the back on my neck stand up.

"I tell you another thing mate, I can't see a scrappy crushing an £80,000 classic car, I would stake my bollocks that even though his lordship has the certificate and paperwork, that car is pugged away somewhere and I'll bloody find it or Mr bloody Majority Salvage will end up in his own crusher."

'Of course, you're bloody right,' I said. "No self-respecting scrappy is going to crush something of that value, they've always got their eyes looking for an earner, it's their heritage, in the blood, they could never pass up an opportunity like that."

"I tell you what," said the inspector, as if he was talking to himself. "I'd better get to our friendly scrappy now, before his lordship gets the same thoughts as us. I lost Thompson, I'm not going to give him a second chance to fuck with our evidence." He rang off.

I called in Mike again.

"Sit down, mate," I said. He sat down and waited; he'd already guessed I had something to say.

"Well, things are beginning to happen, Mike."

"I gathered that boss, but what?"

"Yes I'm sorry, Gary Thompson." I could see the colour drain from his face. "He's dead! I would guess that his lordship started to worry that we were getting close to him, especially when Inspector Densil started to question all of them. And he decided to play safe. I prefer to think that he's panicking and has made a bad mistake. His employees have always remained loyal, which is part of the reason that the police have never been able to get any sort of conviction to stick. How will they feel about this latest turn of events? Hopefully they might start watching their backs and not be so sure of their boss."

I looked at Mike. "How do you feel, mate?"

"I'm fine, I always felt I wanted to be there to watch the bastard die, but now this has happened, I don't mind. The more I learn about this mob the more I realise that everything leads back to his lordship, and he's the one we have got to get, so what's next?"

"Good man, Mike," I said, somewhat relieved. "What I thought now the pressure's on, is that perhaps you should aggravate the situation as only you know how. Perhaps little rumours in the financial pages, hints about a will, the police, questions about murders, a ship without a captain. I don't have to tell you, this is right up your street, you are just the man."

"You leave it to me, boss, I'll have his pips squeaking, and I'll really enjoy it."

"I thought you might, but you just remember they won't take it lying down, they will come after you, so make sure you listen to the boys' downstairs. And be safe, remember you have a future wife to think of."

"Oh bloody hell," he muttered and strode from the room

blushing.

It was, I admit, a source of amazement that a man of the world like Mike undoubtedly could be reduced to a teenage wreck at the mention of the woman he undoubtedly loved to bits. At least it gave me a smile.

CHAPTER TEN (GUARDIAN ANGELS)

I decided to go and check our guardian angels. This is exactly what I thought they would be. Their skill and knowledge was all that stood between the enemy and people that meant a great deal to me.

The problem being that the people that we had to protect were civilians not military, they had no comprehension of how evil people can be to each other, which is why they needed protection from others that did understand. John knew this only too well, which is why he is at Caz's side all the time and will be until this is all over.

I walked into reception and saw exactly what I expected, two young men, six foot plus, obviously fit and although they were not in uniform it was all they could do not to stand to attention and salute me.

These men obviously knew what they were doing. One was stationed behind the reception desk, so it could be used as cover should the need arise. The other stood right across the other side against the wall. This being standard SAS procedure, the principal being the main danger will come from the front door. So you place one man behind the only bit of shelter, to give a bit of protection from, say, a grenade. Your other man with his back to the wall as far away as possible, so he can't be surprised from behind. Therefore any intruders would have to try and deal with two dangerous foes head on, one to the right and another to the far left, very difficult to manage coming through a narrow door whilst being shot at.

"Hello men."

"SIR."

They came over and shook hands, but I noticed their eyes never left the door. It took me back to when I was just like them, you never relax until the job is finished, totally focused.

Which is why the SAS is copied by every special force in the world, and mostly trained by them as well.

I wanted a quiet word with them so tried to usher them into an adjoining room. They followed but one stood in the doorway with it wide open, obviously not happy with the situation, so I went straight into my concerns.

"Look guys," I started.

"SIR."

"Cut out the 'sir' business for a start."

"SIR."

They obviously knew my past, rank, reputation and all that. Maybe from John, maybe just through the regiment, but I decided to give up on the sir business and get on.

"Right men, these people that you're here to look after are civilians, they don't know the world that you do. So remember, don't trust them to do the right thing because there is no telling what reaction they might have to any given situation. I know that you are trained for this type of situation, and you are the best, but these people are mine and I love em all, do you understand what I'm saying?"

"SIR."

Oh gawd! The older-looking one came over to me. "Look sir, John's briefed us and we want you to know, these people are now our people as well and for anyone to do them harm, they will have to go through us to do it, and that won't be easy believe me, OK?"

"OK," I answered.

With that he saluted me, and I bloody saluted him back! But I felt much better, I wouldn't want to take on these two, that's for sure.

CHAPTER ELEVEN (TWO WOMEN)

I decided to walk home across the common. I must admit that it struck me I was doing the very thing that I'd just been telling everybody else not to do. But this was also the place that it all began just a few days ago, and had a strange pull on me. I paused virtually at the spot where Sarah had been mown down. Did I expect to see something? There was nothing, nothing to show the drama of that day, nothing to show the effect that few minutes had already made on a number of lives.

"But we know, don't we David?"

Bloody hell, she was back!

"Can you read my mind?" That would be too bloody much.

"No I can't but we were both thinking the same thing, weren't we?"

"Look, I'm going to try and get Maggie tomorrow, couldn't you stay here and help look after my friends?"

I sat down on a seat overlooking the pond, contemplating that, should anything go wrong, it wouldn't be the nicest thing for her to witness. Here I was trying to spare the feelings of a bloody corpse, do they have feelings? I haven't a clue, but we had a bond, there was no denying that, and I couldn't stop myself from worrying about her and her feelings.

"I can't talk to anyone but you, I chose you, I think, and you're the only one I can communicate with. Sorry, but we are stuck with each other, at least till it's all over.

"That was just an assumption I know, but we'll both find out sooner or later."

"Please don't tell me it could be fucking permanent," I actually said out loud, drawing disapproving glances from a few people within earshot.

"Look, don't bloody ask me, I'm as new to all this as you. I just feel that I'm stuck here until we sort out Maggie. I don't know why, that's just what I feel."

"Oh god, I fucking hope so!"

"So do I, and I wish you'd stop swearing," said Sarah. "Sorry." I'd just apologised to a dead person, perhaps I really was going barmy.

I got up from the seat and carried on home in the early evening sunshine as if I hadn't a care in the world. I did entertain the thought that one would have to be Mother Teresa not to swear in my position.

"Hello!" I shouted, entering my house.

"I'm up here!" Caz answered from upstairs.

I climbed the stairs and heard her in the bathroom. I opened the door and there she was, just out of the bath. I stood watching while she dried herself. I could have stood there watching her all day. I was overcome by the beauty before me. I reached forward, took the towel and started to dry her back. I could smell the dampness of her hair, the softness of her skin and she smelt of warm bath and soap. I've no idea what soap, it didn't matter, it was just her, she always had this effect on me, from the day I first set eyes on her. She turned and looked at me. I don't know if there were tears in my eyes or whether it was just my look.

"Oh David," she said, and she held out her arms to me and we kissed. We made love right there in the bathroom.

We staggered into the bedroom, fighting for breath, and started all over again, a bit more leisurely this time. Afterwards we lay spent and exhausted, a feeling of well-being settled over us. Bathed in post-coital euphoria we dozed off.

I awoke with a start. Caz. was still sleeping, I sat on the edge of the bed pulling on my pants. **"Well done, David!"** It was Sarah.

I leapt up. "What on earth are you doing, can't I have any privacy?"

"Sorry, I can't seem to separate myself from you, it's not my fault."

"You mean you've been here all the time, for the last couple of hours?"

"What do you want, marks out of ten? You obviously did OK, just look at her, women only sleep with that look on their face when they are in love and have just had a good ..."

"Yes, yes, OK, I get the picture."

But I did have a good look at her, she was so beautiful so at peace. I hoped it was partly down to me, but I didn't appreciate anyone giving an opinion on that part of our relationship.

"You really do love her, don't you?" Sarah said quietly. "More than you can ever imagine," I answered. "She came along at a bad time for me and gave me purpose, everything just got better from then on. I don't know if I'd have made it without her. There had been lots of women before her, but there have never been any since the day I met her. Even before we got together, I lost all interest in other women, she was the only thought in my head. I've never told anybody that, I don't think anyone who knows me would believe it. We all have secrets we keep just to ourselves, and here am I telling you."

"I envy you both." She paused. **'It's what we all want, but some of us never find it. You're both very lucky, but I'm sure you know that don't you?"**

"Absolutely I do, I always have."

"I'm sorry, David, because of me it's all been put in jeopardy, I'm so sorry." She sounded very down.

Could dead people feel that sort of emotion? I've no idea, but it seemed so.

"Listen Sarah, there's no point having regrets now, call it fate, kismet, whatever, the one thing I do know is your Maggie is my Maggie too now. I don't know if you transferred these feelings as well, but I will protect her with my life. We can't change that, it's fact, so we've just got to make sure we win."

"Oh thank you David, I could kiss you!"

"I don't think you could," I answered.

"No I can't. I just tried and you didn't feel a thing, not the sort of reaction I'm used to from men in my life, I can assure you."

I couldn't help but smile. "I'm sure you aren't, anything but!" I remembered I had to email Paco, so I moved downstairs to the office, sat at the computer and typed his email address.

CHAPTER TWELVE (THE PAST)

Subject: El Hermano (my brother)

"Who's your brother?" It was Caz. She had woken, come downstairs and was standing behind me in her gown looking at my screen and the email, looking troubled. I waited.

"I have to talk to you," she said. "There's a few things I need answers to. I never question anything you do, you know that, but we are in a different place now and I have a few issues that need answers."

I stood up and held her.

"Firstly, where the bloody hell is John? I'd known there was something wrong but I'd been distracted!"

"John has made his base in the summer house, he can see all round the property from there and he feels it's less intrusive, just as well really!" If only she knew that we had our own companion, more or less permanently at the moment, perhaps later.

I sat her down and said, "Right, I owe you answers to any questions you have, so off you go."

She looked at me thoughtfully.

"I'm not putting pressure on you David, but I love you and something as big as this, I need to know what's going on in your head. I need to share it with you good or bad, do you understand?"

"I think so," was all I could manage.

She took a deep breath and continued.

"Well firstly I know you haven't got a brother, so why the email? Secondly, ever since this happened, the excitement, the danger, you have been like a dog on heat." She did smile at this in spite of

Herself. "It's not that I'm complaining, but it makes me wonder if you've been happy with your life, our life, whether you miss the army that much? "The danger, I suppose, it makes me wonder if you're living the life you want, not just the life you think I want. Do you understand? I know very little of your life before we met and I never ask. I remember what a bad place you were in when we met and the wounds. I thought you would tell me when you were ready, at least I hoped so."I drew a deep breath then opened my mouth.

"It's very difficult.""I'm very sorry if it's too hard," she said.

"It's not that, it's just that you have to face up to things about yourself that maybe other people would never understand, unless they've lived it. But it's personal to you, and you face it, but to tell someone is hard, but I'll try.

"I've wanted to tell you for years, and should have done.

The first thing I want you to know is that

I've never been happier, you are all I want and will ever want, I really do love you and always will. Is that old-fashioned? It sounds it, but it's the truth and I can't even imagine that ever changing so never worry on that account."

"It's not old-fashioned you idiot, it's lovely."

I could see a tear starting to form in her eyes so I pushed on quickly.

"I'll start right back when I left school, it might help you understand. Probably help me as well! I left school after taking my A levels, I did particularly well as a matter of fact."

Caz smiled recognising my usual modesty.

"Anyway, I chose not to go to university, but chose the army, the Royal Marines actually. Don't ask me why, I don't really know or I didn't then.

My parents were totally against it, I was very young

remember so that was enough to convince me.

"Once I joined it was like finding my reason for being, like running a race and finding you could beat everyone with ease. I was a natural, no matter what they asked I loved it and found it easy.

A big thing at that age to find something you really enjoyed. And it never changed. I was fast-tracked with promotions all the way, and within a short time I was captain and was discreetly approached with reference to joining the SAS. I jumped at the chance, again I loved every minute. I passed, even though only about twenty per cent at most make it. This was where I met John Penn.

He was my training sergeant, after all the training we were teamed up as a pair for ops.

"We made a good team and were soon earning a reputation, any and all the crap jobs ended up with us. But we relished it, Ireland, Bosnia, the Gulf, Congo, the list goes on. We were efficient, ruthless and, it seemed, indestructible. Civilians don't realise that it becomes like a drug, the danger, the euphoria when you win, you have to live it to know what it's like.

"We had been living it flat out for a number of years by this time and I think it was beginning to sour somewhat. Looking back, all the killing, being undercover, never knowing if I would survive even till my next meal, it was beginning to take its toll."

I looked in her eyes to see if there was any response. I could see the tears weren't far away, whether this was good or bad I couldn't tell. I decided to plough on.

"The powers that be recognised our ability, if that's the right word, promotions followed. John would never take a commission, he got to sergeant major and that was all he wanted.

"Some time later, we'd just finished a course with the special boat service and returned to Hereford when we were sent for by the CO.

We knocked and entered his office at the command.

'COME.' He was standing with his hands behind his back, fingers interlocked looking out of the window. We heard him tell us to sit which we did. He turned and faced us, he stood about six foot four upright, a handsome man even though he was in his late fifties. Obviously would make a formidable foe even now. This assessing every male you meet is very common in special forces, it's like civilian males assessing rivals for a lady friend. It's an instinct that has been with soldiers since time began.

"He asked, 'So how are you both?' We both answered, 'Fine.' He replied, 'Look I'll get straight to the point, you two have had some rough jobs lately, I do appreciate that believe me, you both deserve a long break.' We waited for the but.

'But I'm sorry we have a nasty little job that we would like you to do, that needs doing really.' We waited.

'It appears that the Italian government has a problem and have asked for our help. They have been clamping down on the Mafia and corruption, with some success I might add, but they have hit a problem. The bad guys have started to kill the judges who are of course in short supply. Honest officials are hard to find. You can understand why, the bribes are enormous, organised crime in Italy is like a religion, everybody is affected, they run or control everything. Which is why the new government decided to do something about it.

"The problem being they don't know what law enforcement people they can trust, the list of trustworthy judges was secret, known to only a few. Someone obviously sold out, consequentially four have already been murdered, one was blown up in his car, with his three children, wife, nanny and chauffeur, all killed.

It was, of course, a message to all the honest judges that want to do the right thing, this is what you risk.

So the government thought if they could get some help from people unknown to the mob with no family to worry about, it would give them an even chance against the killers. The thing is that the majority of the police and the judiciary, even the people, want it sorted but haven't been confident they can be protected."

Caz looked puzzled.

"Why couldn't their own special forces do it?"

"You must remember in those days there weren't many like us. Following the Iranian embassy and Africa, the regiment had legendary status. The Americans and the Israelis had similar, but few others, they were all coming to us for training.

Now everyone has their own special forces but not then.

"Anyhow, I think we were picked because of our reputation and the SBS. Training, we were to go in from the sea, dropped by submarine and swimming in about a mile to a mile and a half.

Of course we ended up going. Armed with a list of targets and of course pictures, pumped up with excitement, adrenalin coursing through our bodies. It was always like this at the beginning of an op. Like I said, it's an addiction, I can't explain it, you have to live it. Even then it's difficult to understand."We swam ashore at night and were met by our two guides, we stowed our suits and flippers and introduced ourselves. My guide was Paco Elvia."

"Paco?" said Caz.

"Yes, the Paco.

There were six targets in all. John took two and I took two. We got going straight away, John going off with his guide and I went off with Paco. Two days later we were all sitting in Paco's village having accounted for all four of them, I told you we were good.

We still had the worst two, one of which was responsible for the car bomb and the massacre of the children and the nanny. Of course, they had now been forewarned by the killing of their compatriots. They would soon link the incidents and realise they were being targeted, which would make them even more dangerous.

"We managed to dismiss all thoughts of this and just sat with Paco, his wife Maria and the kids, eating, drinking and laughing, all the things I'd not enjoyed for years. I never usually envied anybody, but that night I saw something that I truly did envy. Paco with his wife and boys truly in love, truly happy, it came as quite a shock to me that I felt like this. Looking back now I think I was just growing up; I'd lived in the eternal boys' club for years and was, I think, just growing out of it.

"But to me at that time I felt suddenly that I'd wasted my life, all the killing, hiding, fighting was all wrong. I was very young and everything had to be in black and white. I never considered my life decisions in those days, everything was impulse, had to be instant. Other of course than on a mission, when I was cold, hard and focused. Can you understand what a dichotomy my life was becoming? Looking back, which I can do now, I was becoming a lost soul, partly because of battle fatigue, partly because of me. I was changing, maturing if you like. I know I was not in a good place and it was creeping up on me without me quite understanding what it all meant."

I noticed she gave a little nod, I hoped in understanding.

"Sometime after midnight we got round to deciding our plans. John would go with his guide, Pepe, after the assassin nicknamed 'El Gato', I would go with Paco after 'Scorpion'.

"John left straight away, even though it was late, after seeing him and Pepe off I went straight to bed.

"I was awoken suddenly by shouting, screaming, all sorts of commotion. I was up and standing with my gun facing the door when it burst open. It was Paco shouting '*Señor, señor!*' How he was not shot I'll never know, with all the noise, the door crashing in, I should have opened up on anyone coming through that door, but didn't. I grabbed him, sat him down and tried to calm him, I was having trouble understanding all his shouting.

After a few seconds he quietened down and I began to grasp what had occurred.

"During the night, his oldest son, Carlos, had been taken, kidnapped, it appeared that a dead scorpion had been left on his pillow. Which left him with no doubt who had taken the boy. He was only eight, just a baby really, but no ordinary eight-year-old as we would find out.

"A Roman general once wrote that in every soldier's life there comes a time when his heart tells him something entirely different to what his head is telling him. This is his moment of decision! This was mine, I felt enormous guilt, that I was to blame for Carlos being taken. I managed to sit Paco and Maria down at last, I needed to talk to them both.

"I asked them what they wanted to do, me to do specifically. Did they want the police involved? They turned to each other and talked quietly, finally they turned to me and said, 'We know this man is evil, we are sure that he has taken Carlos just to gain some time. We know he will kill him as soon as he thinks he is safe. We don't trust the police, we trust you. We need to get to him and stop him, this is the only chance our boy has got. We know the truth, we are not blind to his situation, but he is only eight and I need to help him. I'm his Papa, he will be looking for me.'

"I told them I would do everything I could to get him back safe and I meant it. Even though my head told me my job was just to stop the Scorpion, Carlos was just collateral damage.

But I was being driven by my heart for the first time and I would do everything in my power to bring him home safe.

"I managed to calm them down and to focus on what we had to do if Carlos was to have a chance, which was becoming more and more important to me every minute.

"We left within half an hour and moved up into the mountains. We managed to pick up his trail almost straight away, courtesy of Carlos I'm sure, although I didn't mention anything to his dad.

"But his dad was a man born and bred in these mountains and had quickly realised what was happening. He said, 'Carlos has spent his short life with me in these mountains, he is at home here and has knowledge beyond his years.' I can tell that he is leaving just enough signs to show us the way without getting caught, let's hope he stays careful, eight-year-olds are not known for patience.'"He will,' was all Paco said then he went quiet again.

"We kept up a good pace, helped by the odd branch broken, the odd piece of material from Carlos's shirt, the odd cut on a tree. This boy certainly had his wits about him. By now I knew I had to save him, it had become an obsession. I think I saw it as enabling me in some way to make recompense for some of the things I'd done which I was now beginning to have doubts concerning the efficacy or morality of.

"By the second day we were getting very close, I stopped Paco and sat him down.

'We are close now, any time he is going to spot us, we

must separate, it will give us double the chance of getting Carlos. I want you to go up there into the high ground.' I signalled where I meant, pointing out a rocky summit to the hill which ran parallel to our trail. 'You follow me from those rocks, keep out of sight, if he knows you're there he will start shooting, do you understand?'"It is my son we are talking about, I understand. I have been hunting these mountains all my life, even I won't know I'm there.'"I was sure then that he was focused on what he had to do, up till then I wasn't sure if he could control the emotions that he must be feeling. But he had and he was ice cold. I knew I could rely on him, I certainly wouldn't want him hunting me. 'Right, once I catch up to him I will try to negotiate with him for Carlos, this should hopefully draw him out from cover, whatever happens, as soon as I've got Carlos, he's yours.'

"I handed him my sniping rifle, it was the latest, an L115A.338 British made in Portsmouth, I'd better not mention a name, but it had a range in excess of a thousand metres and could even fire armour-piercing shells. It was not officially in production as yet but we had been given a couple to test in the field and so far we loved it.

"He took it without hesitation, familiarised himself with it and he was gone, with just a mumbled 'Si'. Within seconds I had lost sight of him. I was more than happy he wouldn't let me down, this was his ground, he was born and bred in these mountains, it was home. He also wanted the Scorpion more than anything except maybe his son.

"I'd seen this in his eyes back at the village, he felt it was a personal insult, the assumption that he would back off to save his son, you could see where the culture of 'vendetta' lies in the psyche of the Italian male. He would not relent until his honour was satisfied. I was actually relying on this to give me some small chance of maybe surviving the next few hours. I would be doing my best to save his son, and hope he was good enough to perhaps save me. I moved off, trying not to provide a target, but I did want him to know I was there. I hadn't travelled far before I spotted him. He was sightly ahead of me hidden in a group of trees, holding Carlos in front of him. I got the feeling that he felt somewhat uneasy, unsure of what

I might do. I could feel this from his body language, a skill gleaned from years of conflict, where your life can depend on your ability to read an opponent's body language. I hoped that I'd retained enough of this skill "He stepped slightly from his cover, just enough to let me see him.

I held my hands up with my M16, then I laid it on the floor, he moved forward a few more steps feeling a bit more confident now that I'd put my weapon down. He would surmise that I would have a handgun, but would know that a handgun would not present the same threat as a carbine at that range. So hopefully he was feeling pretty cocky and thinking he was winning.

"That was just what I wanted him to think, he obviously didn't know about Paco or he would never have ventured out from cover.

"I shouted to him, 'All I want is the boy, give me him unhurt and you can be on your way, and I will not follow. Hurt him and I will follow you forever or until you are dead.'"He thought for a moment.

'I will trust you.' He pulled Carlos to him and spoke in his ear, then he shouted, 'I will send the boy over if you give me your word.'""I do,' I replied. I knew he had no intention of letting either of us live, just wanted me in the open watching the boy and not him.

"Carlos moved nervously towards me; he was keeping right out in the open as he had obviously been instructed. I gestured to him to keep coming and to try to move nearer the trees. He was frightened, I could tell, he'd probably been told that he would be shot if he didn't stay out in the open away from cover. I moved slightly nearer the trees, every inch would be an advantage when the bullets started to fly. I tried to move closer to Carlos without our friend noticing.

"'I'll wish you god's speed as soon as he gets to me, my friend.' I was really trying to distract him, all the time trying to edge nearer and nearer to Carlos. He waved, all the time smiling like a predator that had its prey assured.

"'When I shout NOW Carlos, dive to the floor, as flat as you can and as near to the trees as you can.' He blinked his eyes to let me know he understood, all the time getting closer and closer.

"I now had to watch our friend, his every move, I had to time my move just right or we would have no chance of surviving. I could see the sweat dripping from his face even from this distance: he was now very nervous. He knew I was dangerous but without my M16 he couldn't see me as a threat, he probably thought I believed him when he said he would let Carlos go, it gave him the confidence to wait for just the right moment. Of course he didn't know about Paco, hopefully. Carlos was now only about ten feet away from me and the time was now. I watched our friend, my eyes boring into him, I saw him wipe his hand on his jacket, they were obviously damp from sweat, he started to lift his carbine. This was it. 'NOW!' I shouted, drew my pistol and started firing, not with much hope of doing any damage but you never know and it might distract his aim.

"I had seen Carlos hit the ground, he had actually dived towards the cover, this boy was a natural. I ran to him as our friend opened fire, he had missed, I dived on top of him just as I felt a burning in my leg, he had hit me. I dragged, rolled, threw, the boy into cover, all the time firing my pistol in the general direction of the Scorpion.

"I felt what I knew to be a couple more hits, but we were now in cover and the boy was unhurt.

"'You OK?' He nodded. I noticed there were no tears, he was his father's son!"I checked for wounds. I had been hit in the leg, one bullet had hit me in the side of my neck or shoulder, I couldn't be sure, and one had hit me in the right side just below my ribs, but had gone right through. None were fatal as far as I could tell but I had to survive the next few minutes first.

"I asked Carlos if he could see anything, he said he couldn't. I surmised that matey was not taking any chances, he would know that he had hit me, but wouldn't know how bad so was taking his time.

"'Where's Papa?' "'He's here, just wait'.

"I heard our friend moving, he had decided it was time to finish us off and was making his way towards us. I didn't think I could roll over to face him without crying out in pain, which would give our location away. I managed to roll on my side so I could reload. I'd fired all twenty rounds in the fracas. I put a new magazine in, I realised that the bullet that had hit my leg had broken the bone and was bloody agony.

"I lifted my arm slightly.

'Can you see him?' I said to Carlos. '*Si sta andando verso di noi*' (he is coming straight for us).

"I lifted the gun, trying to enable me some sort of shot at him. Pain shot through my leg, I was close to passing out. I must have made some sort of grunt because I heard him stop and listen then move on, whether in a different direction I couldn't tell, but he was getting nearer.

"Carlos took my hand, holding the gun in his two hands he pointed it, taking aim, his face was set like a grown man.

'*Posso farlo*' (I can do it) he said, meaning he could aim and I could pull the trigger."'Are you sure?'"'*Si*,' came his reply.

"What choice did we have, if Paco didn't act we were sitting ducks.

"'Can you see him?' I asked.

"'*Si sta andando verso di noi*.' (he is heading straight for us)"'Wait as long as you can, we will only get one chance,' I whispered.

"He was looking along the barrel taking sight.

"'We wait till he lifts his gun to point at us, aim for his chest.'"I figured that was the largest target, if we could hit him and put him down, who knows?"'I'm sure I could hear his breathing now, my finger started to squeeze the trigger in anticipation of his shout. I had already made up my mind to empty half the magazine in the general direction that Carlos was aiming, not with too much optimism, we had no choice, then I would roll over and let him have the rest, by then it wouldn't matter if I screamed.

'*Si Si dai Scorpione*.' (Yes, yes come scorpion.) Carlos was lost in concentration.

"'*Si Si*,' he whispered.

"I heard a thud, Carlos jumped back, a shocked expression registered on his face. '*Mis di mio dio eandatolui*.' (My god he's gone.)"I swung myself over to face the direction he should be, my pistol held out in front. I'd let out a scream of pain which I figured no longer mattered. I looked over the area in front of me, I couldn't see anything. I took another careful look, I knew he must be there, slowly I covered the ground in front of us. Then I spotted what I guessed was the Scorpion lying in the grass. Where his head had been there was just a bloody mass, Paco's bullet had entered his skull just above the bridge of his nose, right in the centre of the forehead. It had exited, taking the whole of his skull with it. He couldn't have known a thing. What a shame, I would have delighted in him experiencing some extreme pain, never mind!

"Carlos was shaking, he had been through more than most grown men could take. I took hold of him and gave him a squeeze, held him close. 'We're safe now, sunshine.' He sobbed violently for a few minutes, then that was it, he was over it, a real tough kid that one.

"'What happened?' he said.

"'Your papa, I told you he was here.'

"He looked around. 'But where?'

"'He'll be along soon, did he have any medical kit?' gesturing towards our deceased friend.

"'I think so, I'm not sure.'

"'You pop up to where he was hiding and have a look, I could really do with some medical help.' I thought it would help him to be busy.

"'*Si*' and he was off like a rabbit.

"I started to check my wounds more carefully. I was right, one bullet had passed through my right side, so shouldn't be too much of a problem. There was a lot of blood round my neck but I didn't think that was too much of a problem either. My leg was the biggest problem, the bullet had broken the tibia and would therefore bleed a lot into my leg. The bullet was still in there somewhere, without medical help it could be a major problem and we were in the middle of nowhere.

"I could hear Paco approaching, also I could feel myself getting lightheaded, I fought against it as much as I could. Paco arrived and knelt next to me.

"'We are brothers forever, I saw what you did, you took the bullets meant for Carlos. I apologise, I couldn't get a clear shot until he came for you.'"You certainly took the right shot then, *muchos gracias*. It was this rifle, I love it, It's god's avenging arm.' He crossed himself in that delightful

90

Latin style.

"'It's yours, you keep it. It'll remind you of me.'

"'We will never forget you, I told you we are brothers, I can never repay the debt I owe you.'"'Listen Paco, your son is a son to be proud of, I told you we would get him back.' My head was beginning to spin again as Carlos got back with a bag, there was a brief hug between them and then back to business. They tipped out all sorts of medical paraphernalia, I was desperately trying to keep my consciousness.

"'Show me the drugs.' I looked at what he held out.

I selected one I thought was an antibiotic, well it ended in 'cillin'.

Whether it was suitable I hadn't a clue, but I was by now desperate. God knows how long before I got proper treatment. I filled a syringe with what I hoped was the right amount, then looked for a vein. I was showing Paco how to clear the air and give the injection. I didn't think I'd be conscious for long and hoped Paco could manage it.

"Carlos was trying to talk to me, his dad stood and was trying to get things ready to leave. He realised the situation was serious and wanted to be on the move. 'What's the trouble son?' I could see he was worried.

"'I found something in his bags,' he said, looking about him nervously.

"'What did you find?'

"'I found money, a lot of money,' he said.

"I wasn't that surprised, he was doing a runner so couldn't do a bank transfer really, could he. 'Look Carlos, you hide it right, don't tell anyone. If I make it, come and see me and we'll sort it out. If I don't, you tell your papa, quietly, but for now keep it secret and don't worry, OK?'

"'*Sí*'.

"Paco had obtained some sticks and was busy splinting

my leg.

"'Paco, one thing before I black out, I shot him, not you, that way there will be no repercussions, you don't want people looking for revenge or whatever. They will never be able to find me. Even if they could, they would soon regret it.' He nodded. It made sense and he knew it.

"He began strapping my leg and I finally gave in to the inevitable and drifted off into oblivion. Over the next day or so, I can't be sure as I must have been drifting in and out of consciousness, but I realised that Paco was carrying me on his back. How? I don't know, I'm not a small man.

"As far as I can gather during that first twenty hours, they only stopped to drink and to inject me. Eventually Paco virtually collapsed so they had little choice but to stop and rest.

"I could hear them talking but I was too far gone to understand a word. I learnt subsequently that they had decided we were going too slow, they had tried my mobile several times to no avail, no signal in these mountains. It was agreed that Carlos would go ahead as fast as he could, till he reached the bridge where we had crossed the river on the way up. Paco was fairly certain he would get a signal there, he could then contact John and he would do the rest.

"Failing this, he would have to keep running until he got a signal or reached the village, either way Paco would get to the bridge and wait for rescue. It had been decided that the bridge was about as far as his strength would last, and mine!"I don't remember much more until I heard lots of noise which I now know to be the helicopter.

The next thing I remember was paramedics all over me, drips going in, oxygen masks, drugs wounds being dressed, thank god for unconsciousness, the blackness that takes away all pain.

"Next time I awoke I was in a hospital bed, tubes in

every orifice, well it seemed like it, surrounded by all the paraphernalia of medical technology. I had survived!

"'How are you feeling?' said my nurse.

"Well apart from being shot until I resembled a colander, leg tied together with a bit of tree and my belt then carried down a mountain, nothing to eat for god knows how long. I feel fine! 'Not bad thanks,' was my stock reply. 'You tell me, how am I?'"

'Well,' she said, 'you'll survive, it will take a bit of time, but you will be as good as new eventually. Thanks in no small part to your friend over there, who I understand carried you from the mountains.'"I looked to where she was pointing. I could see Paco with the obligatory tubes lying in bed.

"'What's the matter with him? Is he OK?'

"'He'll be fine, he's suffering from exhaustion, carrying you all that way. It's a wonder it didn't kill him.'""Not him love, it would take a lot more than that to kill him, and have you met his son yet?'"Then I was gone back into the wonderful blackness.

I was deep in thought, in my own world of memory, when I noticed Caz. She was also deep in her own thoughts. She put her arms round me and held me, I don't know for how long we stayed like that. I think until she thought I was ready to go on. I looked at my watch. I had been talking for an hour and a half. My whole self felt drained, as much for facing my own demons as for telling it all to someone else.

"I've never told anyone what happened on that mountain, but I do know I wasn't trying to end it all."

"What about the things you'd done, do you still feel they were wrong?"

"No, I know now that the things we did, the people we killed, they were all killers, mostly they had kidnapped innocent Brits, and we were sent to rescue them, I know one thing for sure, none of the people we rescued thought we did anything wrong."

"Nor do I darling, I know you could never be bad, it's just not in you."

"I came to terms with all that lying in that hospital all those years ago, and I've never had a sleepless night since. Call it post traumatic stress, battle fatigue, whatever, soldiers have always suffered because of it and always will, I suppose, perhaps I was lucky, I met you."

"That goes both ways," said Caz. "Anyway, what happened to Paco and Carlos? And the money?"

"Well Paco went home the next day. I was still in and out of consciousness but aware enough to know what was going on, days moved on and I began to feel better. Paco and Carlos had visited but I think Paco judged that I was not ready to start making decisions, so I took the initiative and came out with it.

"'Did Carlos tell you about the money?'

"'Yes,' he answered.

"'So what do you think?'

"'I did think we should give it to the police, but now I'm not so sure, which is why I waited till I could talk to you, this sort of thing is your world, it's not something I understand.'

"I looked at Paco, I had to get him out of this.

"'I think there is only one thing you can do, hang on to the money. If you hand it in, the bogey men will know within minutes. If you spend any, the bogey men will know, if you tell a soul, they will find out. This is what you do, you hide the money, you bring the bag to me, secretly.

I will make a show of handing it over to my authorities, they already think I killed him, so they will quite readily accept that I would have his booty.'

"'But they will come after you.'

"'Listen Paco, I'm paid for this, you have a family, you must think of them first.'"He looked at me resigned, he knew I was right, but he wasn't happy, his Latin blood wanted him to stand side by side with his brother and get slaughtered of course. No wonder they were not good at wars, not ruthless enough! Well not since Roman times. 'Look I'll be back in Hereford in a few days, they won't be stupid enough to try and come after me there, in the meantime I'll get a couple of chaps to stand guard, I'll be fine.

Then in a few months time you can put about a rumour that an uncle had died and left you his farm wherever, then discreetly move and you will be free. Just contact me when you are ready and I can get it done for you in secret so it can never be traced.'"You can do that?'

"'Yes, no problem.' I just hoped I could!"That's what happened. I returned to the UK, a few days later I met you, she was my physio, my life began again from there.

"Paco bought his place in Spain some six months later, which was all arranged in secret, I couldn't do it but I knew a man who could. Which worked because he's lived there in peace ever since.

"And now you know my life story, more or less!""What happened to Carlos and how much money was there? You can't tell just half a story," she said, nudging me in the ribs. "Typical man."

"Right, I don't know how much money, cos I never asked, but he once said when I started the firm, if I wanted to borrow the odd million or so euros just to ask!. As for Carlos, he's studying for a degree in aeronautical engineering, and is a fine lad, as I think will be his brother."I looked at her, trying to assess how she felt.

"Thank you for telling me," she said. "I did wonder about a few things and it's so nice to know things from before I was around. You managed to talk for over three hours without a mention of any females.""I lived the life of a monk until we met!"

She just smiled and kissed me.

CHAPTER THIRTEEN
(THE GAME'S AFOOT)

We awoke to the ringing of the phone. We had both crashed out early the previous evening, I suppose the emotions had taken their toll because we slept solidly until interrupted by the phone.

"Hello," I mumbled. It was Mike.

"They've arrested his lordship! It was just on the news. I got a big spread in the FT suggesting that he could lose control of the company. The shares will dive when the markets open." The joy in his voice you could feel.

"Great, perhaps he'll forget about me for the next few days. Somehow I doubt it, he will probably be more dangerous, so you listen to your minders. But try and keep the pressure on while I'm away.""You leave it to me boss, god I feel so good." And he put the phone down.

"I'm glad you're not my enemy." Sarah was here.

"There's still time sweetie."

"Don't you sweetie me," she said.

"Was that story last night all true?" she continued.

"What do you think?"

It seems like I no longer questioned her being there and being a party to everything n my life.

"I'm sure it's true, I'm just so glad I chose you to help Maggie."

"Listen my dear, number one, how do you get that you chose me? I think you grabbed the first poor soul available, if grab is the right word. Secondly, how do you know I'm the right one to help Maggie?"

"I know, all right."

"Is this your other woman?" It was Caz.

She must have been listening to this peculiar conversation. **"You tell her I'd give her a fight if it were possible,"** said Sarah.

"What are you smiling at Mr?" She nudged me in the ribs. I'm sure she knew.

"You just make sure you tell her that you are spoken for, matey!"

"You tell her she's loved by you all right, of that I'm certain (sigh) never mind."

Just how bizarre this situation was seemed to be passing us by, and total acceptance had taken over.

"She says that I love you."

"You think that a woman doesn't know when she's loved?" said Caz.

I looked at her and said, "Your sex has an even worse record than mine for being deceived by the opposite gender. True?"

She looked me in the eye. "Not this one, my friend."

"I knew I'd like her." Sarah again.

"You be bloody quiet."

"She agrees, doesn't she?" said Caz.

This was a nightmare, two women ganging up on me, one of whom it would appear that I had no escape from.

"There is something I would like to ask Sarah," said Caz. "What's that?" said Sarah.

"You obviously love your daughter, therefore, if you did nothing after you were … you know."

"Killed right?"

"Yes so if you had done nothing to protect her, she would have been killed and you could have been together again."

There was a prolonged silence, then Sarah spoke.

"Don't believe for one minute that it didn't cross my mind, I miss her so much, but she's young beautiful, intelligent and hasn't lived at all as yet, because we were always hiding. But I soon realised that it was my job to make sure she got her chance at life, what she does with that chance is up to her, but I know I've got to try and give her that chance, do you understand?" I had been passing this on to Caz as it was being said. I could see tears running down her cheeks

"I was hoping that's what she would say. I don't want you risking your life for the wrong reasons."

"I knew I would like her, you would never choose anyone who wasn't lovely, I just knew."

"Sarah likes you," I said. "And I like her," was the reply.

I had to now get myself organised. I was hoping that the trouble his lordship was getting from the law would preoccupy his thoughts and give me a slight advantage time wise, to get Maggie back.

His lordship would be very aware that should I get Maggie back and to a lawyer, we had won, well not quite won, but his chances of hanging on to complete control of the company would have been made, to say the least, very difficult. So I knew his aim was to kill her if at all possible, and my demise would be just a bonus.

I arrived at the office to be greeted by a despondent looking Mike.

"What's up mate?" I said.

"They've let him go, pending further investigations," Mike snapped.

"Listen Mike, it was always only Charlie Densil putting on the pressure, this is just the beginning, we're going to get him, all we have to do is survive."

"Yes I know, it was just seeing him in handcuffs, it was

like all my dreams coming true."

"I know what you mean, but we want him to feel the pressure, he's never had any trouble from anyone before, well, not like we are going to give him anyway."

"Fair enough, oh by the way, Charlie Densil tried to phone you earlier, said he would try again."

I picked up the phone and dialled Charlie's number, it rang and Charlie answered. "Hello Davey."

"Hello Charlie," I responded. He knew I was anxious to get down to business, so he wasted no more time.

"Right, we visited our scrappy friend and after a frank and forthright of views he decided to see it my way, and we got the Bentley. There are a few bits, unimportant bits to us, missing, but as we speak our forensic looneys are examining every nut and bolt on that vehicle. If anyone has broken wind in that motor in the last twenty years, they will give us their name and address and date of birth."

"How long will it take, Charlie?"

"Probably a couple of days. We've also got the CCTV tapes from the hospital, if we can spot one of his employees I will bring them all in. I will squeeze the life out of them, I'm sure they are having doubts about their boss, wouldn't you? We will get him, I've got a feeling this time."

"I hope you're right Charlie," I said. "I really do."

We said our goodbyes, I noticed Mike standing by the door, he looked devastated.

"They've got the Bentley?" he said quietly. "All they need now is to find bits of Sammie's family on it and maybe we can get him."

What a terrible thought, I had never quite thought of it in those terms before.

"Mike, I'm sorry mate I never realised you were still in the room."

"No, it's OK, it's what I want, just the thought of people searching, looking for bits of Sean and young Jake that's all, they were family to me as you know."

I walked over to him and put my arm around his round his shoulder, he was as white as a ghost. I sat him in my chair and said, "You stay here as long as you want, I'll make sure you are not disturbed." As I closed the door I thought I heard a sob, I wondered how long he had loved Sammie. I stationed young Mary to watch the door. Nothing would get past her, she was only small but when she had a mission she was formidable. I'm sure she knew what was going on, how I haven't a clue, but she never missed a thing.

I made the indispensable cup of tea and headed towards my office, the door opened, Mike was on his way out looking as if nothing was wrong.

"I made this for you, come in and shut the door.""I'm all right boss, it was just the thought of them scraping about for bits of people you love. We grew up together Sean and me, inseparable, we went to the same uni." He paused.

"Even fell for the same girl." Christ he'd said it.

"We did all know, did Sean?"

"Yes of course, we even talked about it once, it didn't worry him, he knew I would never try to take it further and I think it just worried him that I never stuck with any of my girlfriends for long. He thought it was because of my feelings for Sammie."

"And was it?"

"Probably, I never thought much about it at the time, but I never felt anything for them like I felt for her."

"She does know you know".

"I'm not sure, it just feels like I'm trying to benefit from his death."

"Look Mike, I'm sure she feels the same as you, think of

the time you're wasting."

"I can't do anything until this is all over."

You can't make people do things until they're ready, so I left it, they will get round to it given time.

I arrived at Blackbushe Airport a little late. I didn't want to hang around and risk people noticing I wasn't Jay, so Mike dropped me right along side the Cessna, then drove straight off. I jumped into the plane, got into the pilot's seat, put on my headset sunglasses and a baseball cap for good measure, even my mother would find it hard to know who it was.

"Tower to bandit, tower to bandit."

"Bandit to tower, what the bloody hell is up with you, you old bugger." This was my best Jay impression, would it do?"Tower to bandit, where are you off to in such a rush? I bet it's a woman."

"Bandit to tower, you know better than that Bill, you nosey old sod, but I am in a hurry, so I'll tell you all about it when I get back, can I bloody go now out."

"OK mate if you're in that much of a hurry, the fight plan and paperwork is all done so piss off."

"Cheers Bill me old mate, see you in a couple of days. I'll bring you back a case of the best Italian red."

I opened the throttles and both engines roared, I surged forward down the runway before anything could delay me. Both engines purred beautifully and within seconds the wheels left the ground and I was climbing up into the clouds on my way, to where and into what, that remained to be seen. The radio crackled. "You all right Jay?" Bill had sensed something was not quite right.

"Yes mate I'm fine, I'll explain all when I get back, over and out."

I swept up through the clouds and turned south, the auto pilot had all been set up by Jay, so as soon as I could I engaged it and relaxed.

I still had an overwhelming feeling that things were only just beginning, and what had gone before was nothing to what was to come. The famous phrase from Sherlock Holmes kept coming into my head over and over – THE GAME'S AFOOT. To be honest I must admit to a great feeling of excitement, the next few days would determine all of our futures.

The next three hours disappeared in what seemed like minutes. I was nearing my destination and had dropped down to avoid being seen on radar. Flying through these mountains needed concentration, but I picked up the radio. "Brother, brother."

"*Ola, mi hermano,*" Paco's reply.

"Minutes" then I cut off, I wanted the minimum of airtime just in case someone was listening.

I turned the plane into the valley where I could now see Paco's farm and airstrip. It looked just as beautiful as I remembered nestled in the valley between mountains, the land green and lush, in contrast to the mountains and surrounding countryside which was dry and parched, the image that tourists are accustomed to seeing on their holidays in sunny Spain. This little valley however was a little touch of paradise, fertile soil, sheltered from the harshest sun, an endless supply of water. In fact, a perfect climate, he grew everything he wanted on this farm – fruit, vegetables, livestock – and of course he was happy. I always have this same reaction every time I fly into the valley, and it always takes me by surprise.

I felt the wheels touch down and braked until I was down to walking pace. I could see Paco and the family waiting for me by the second little hangar.

I turned the plane and slowly made my way into the

hangar, out of sight should anybody be looking or even flying over trying to spot my plane.

I came to a halt, switched everything off and started to climb out. I opened the side door and made my way down the steps; the family were all there to greet me in the customary Latin way – embraces, kisses, tears, all slightly embarrassing to a true Brit but I had to admit, if only to myself, to enjoying it. We made our way to the house. I knew we would have to enjoy a full meal plus several bottles of wine before any talk of business, so I just relaxed and went with it. Being with Paco and his family was always pleasure and something I enjoyed.

Finally Paco said, "Shall we go outside for a smoke and a chat?" Which was his way of saying, 'let's get down to the reason you are here'.

I followed him outside and we sat on a wall. "What is it this time, *mi amigo*, and how can I help?' "I've come to get someone out, quietly! A young girl actually, eighteen, I've got to meet her at Grazalema in the mountains."

"I know it well, quite a walk from here, all up hill and rugged, shouldn't be a problem for you, but a young girl?" "She's lived here most of her life and if she's anything like her mum, I'll struggle to keep up."

"She's walked these mountains all of her life, you'll never keep up." Sarah was here.

I showed no reaction to being spoken to by a bloody ghost, Paco just could never handle that.

"There is a shepherds' track all the way, easy to follow, what else do you need?"

"What I need is an automatic pistol, a common or garden hunting rifle and a lightweight tent in case the weather blows up at altitude. How long should it take us to get there?"

"You should do it in two days with ease, that should get

you there by lunchtime on the second day.

It's only about fifty to sixty kilometres but all climbing up to about fifteen hundred metres on the way there, just a stroll for you even though you're getting on a bit!"

"At least it will be downhill all the way back, for my old bones," I retorted.

Paco just laughed.

"When do you want to leave?" he asked.

"First thing in the morning, if you've got the hardware."

"I've got it, I guessed what you would want, you soldiers never change the weapons you like. It's like a comfy pair of boots. It's what you've always got to have otherwise you don't feel right. I got a Sig. Sauer P226, with a twenty round mag, right?"

"Perfect," I replied.

"If you don't mind Paco, I'd prefer to keep all this to ourselves.

The people who are after me are not nice and will kill both me and the girl if they find us. They have already killed the girl's mother, and a good few others.

I know I can trust the family, but if someone finds out I've landed here and they are questioned, they can answer truthfully if they don't know anything."

"*Si*, it will be as you wish."

"*Gracias,*" I answered and we made our way back to the family.

I slept like a log and awoke at dawn and was ready to go as the sun broke over the mountains.

Carlos was waiting for me with the kit bag and rifle. "I will take you to the path, it's easy from there."

We slowly began to climb, steadily up and up, the view back down to the valley became more and more stunning the higher we climbed. After about two hours we stopped for a drink."What's up Carlos?"

I'd sensed that something was bothering him ever since we left the farm.

"Is Papa in danger? I remember danger always followed you when I was a boy.""Believe me Carlos, I'd do anything to safeguard your father, in fact all of you, I truly believe there is no danger, but we can never be completely sure, so you and Paco do whatever you need to do to make sure you stay safe, that's all I can tell you."He nodded his head and just said, "*Gracias mi hermano.*' It wasn't until later that I realised that I'd spoken Spanish the whole time I'd been with them and they hadn't questioned it once. "The track is there, it is easy to follow and will lead you right to Grazalema, and may god be with you."I walked up the track as quickly as I could. What would I do if I had brought them danger, I just wanted to get moving, to be on my own and to stop worrying about what could happen if things were to go wrong.

I carried on walking for a good few hours. I figured I must be about two thirds of the way to Grazalema and meeting Maggie. I decided to make camp and eat, it would by then be getting close to the time that I said, I would pick up emails on my phone, god I hope I could remember how.

The tent went up in seconds and I settled down with my meat, bread and fruit, there was even a bottle of wine courtesy of Maria, I would guess, but very welcome. I was still thinking about Carlos and what he had said, but I had to live with it, so I decided to forget it.

"You can't worry about everyone you know," Sarah said.

"I can't help it, so how did you know?"

"It is written all over your face, just remember Paco, Carlos, probably the whole family would already be dead, if it wasn't for one lone soldier who

put himself out there to save a family of strangers.

Do you think that Paco doesn't already know that? He would be by your side at the drop of a hat and would count it a privilege so to do, and you know it."

"I know soldiers shouldn't have time to think. It's not good for them, where have you been anyway?"

"Why, have you missed me?"

"Are you joking," I answered, but I had to confess to myself that I had missed her, even the embarrassment of knowing someone was sharing every personal, private detail of my life with me seemed to matter less.

I checked my emails. The only message was, 'NO PROBLEMS'. That was a relief.

"Well your ladyship, we meet your girl tomorrow." There was silence, then she said,

"I hope she's OK."

"Are you nervous?" I asked.

"You see you don't have to be able to see people to know what they are thinking, do you?"

"Don't you worry Sarah, we'll get her out safe," I said. "Or we'll all be meeting very soon."

"I know what you're thinking," she snapped.

It was dark now so I rolled over and went straight to sleep. I'm to old for these mountain walks.

CHAPTER FOURTEEN (ATTACK)

Although I was not a personal witness to the events in this chapter, I have spent many hours with all involved and have related all the facts with complete accuracy. John was nervously pacing round my house, darkness was just beginning to descend, night would not be long. John was uneasy, soldiers of John's experience, so I'm told, get a feeling or a sense of impending action. Whether it's true or not I can't prove, but just ask any old soldier who's seen action and you will only get one answer.

Anyway, John definitely wasn't comfortable that evening.

He had received a call earlier from Bill Meeks, he was expecting it because I'd told him his story and he agreed he sounded just what we needed. They had agreed to meet for a chat whenever Bill was free and said goodbye.

John and Caz had eaten and watched some television, but John was filled with apprehension and couldn't shake it. It was getting late now and Caz got up and said she was off to bed, but feeling John's tension she said, "What's troubling you, John?"

"I don't know, just an old soldier's feelings, I'd like you to take this, just in case."

He handed her a small pistol; he could feel her draw back. "Just for me, please."

She took it reluctantly. He showed her how to release the safety catch and said, "You just point and pull the trigger, it might just save your life."

She walked up the stairs to bed without a backward glance.

John returned to check his weaponry; he would not be going to bed tonight that was for sure. He settled down in an armchair to wait.

He obviously dosed off because his next sensation was his phone vibrating in his pocket. He answered it.

"Hello."

"Bill Meeks, your perimeter has been breached." "How many?"

"Four maybe five, all in black with night goggles." "Cheers Bill."

"I'll check their car and then I'll try and back you up." "Make sure you're wearing a light shirt, I don't want to shoot you by mistake."

"Right, and good luck mate." He was gone.

John took one last check of the room, picked up a little plunger he'd prepared and crouched behind the bar and waited completely calm now, ready for the fray.

There was complete silence or so it seemed to John, like time was suspended, the silence seemed to go on forever as he sat there waiting. Of course it wasn't, it just felt that way.

John could feel sweat beginning to run down his forehead, then he heard a slight noise, it was the sliding door of the house. He decided to take a look, even though he knew it was risky, slipped on his night vision goggles, and slowly lifted his head above the bar. He saw immediately that two were coming in the back and two in the front, all wearing night vision goggles.

They had spotted John even though he only exposed the tip of his head above cover and a couple had opened fire.

John felt something hit him at the top of his shoulder, he knew he hadn't been shot but thought it was probably splinters from the bar, this was it.

They now thought this was going to be easy and, full of

confidence, walked into the room together.

John closed his eyes and pressed the plunger. The plunger operated four flashlights simultaneously. The one drawback with night vision gear is that it's very light sensitive, so setting off the flashlights with them in the room looking straight at him, would temporarily blind them. This was all the advantage John would need, hopefully.

John opened his eyes and stood up. He could see them thrashing about in confusion trying to clear their eyes. He bought up both pistols and opened fire. The two front men dropped instantly, John had put two bullets in their chest followed by one in the head in case they were wearing body armour.

The few seconds was just enough to enable the other two to start shooting, although they still couldn't see properly, they fired wildly in John's general direction. He returned fire with the man to his right hitting him twice in the chest. It was obvious that he was not wearing body armour as his chest exploded, with blood and tissue redecorating that section of the room, signalling that he no longer posed any threat.

John turned his attention to the remaining gunman to his left. The fraction of a second while John had been busy had enabled the gunman to regain some composure, his sight would not be back completely, but he would now start to make out where he was and where he could take cover to avoid this man's deadly fire.

They fired simultaneously. John felt a blow to the right side of his chest, it occurred to him that this must be what it felt like to be hit with a sledgehammer. He was wearing a vest, but the force of the two bullets knocked him completely flat on his back and in severe pain. His head was spinning, he was barely conscious, he knew he had to get his senses back, and quick.

He was not worried about any injury, it was painful, but not serious. But Meeks had said five, he had only got four, assuming that he'd hit the last one, he was fairly certain that he had hit him but he would need to make sure. Then of course there was the other man, the fifth man, this would be the danger man.

He had sent the others in to see what fire power we had, while he waited, standing out there in the shadows waiting his chance, yes this was the one to worry about.

John forced himself to stand, reload his weapons and check the room, section by section. He could see nothing moving, but was now fully aware. There was an enemy in the room, who, might at this moment be stalking him, he thought he had hit him when they both fired, but couldn't be sure. So until he could verify it one way or the other, he had to assume he was still active.

He decided that if his shots had missed then he must be behind the settee by the door into the garden. But how to find out without getting shot, that was the problem right now.

John made his way slowly and quietly to the far end of the furniture; it took a while but he had to be sure and careful. He could see the feet of number four now, they were not moving. John stood still and watched for a while until he was fairly sure, then he moved to the settee. He could see that number four would not bother anybody again, he had hit him with both bullets, the bullets had hit him in the face. John had actually been aiming for his chest but the action of diving for cover meant that they had both hit him in the face by accident. Ironically, John noticed he was wearing a vest, strange how fate works sometimes.

John now had the last gunman to find. A noise startled him and he spun round. It was Caz on the stairs, she had clicked on a lamp, he rushed to the stairs. "Turn off the lamp, quick!" John knew as he said it she was too late, he felt a bullet smash into his thigh. It threw him across the room, he hit the wall and must have blacked out for a few seconds.

He could then hear Caz screaming, "John, John!" but he couldn't move, he must do something, he must save Caz.

He heard footsteps, number five, he knew even though he couldn't as yet see him. The fifth man was now very sure of himself. "Mr Carey I presume, I thought you would be too good for those four, I was right obviously, I thought I would wait until my chance occurred, and it did."

John could see him now, he was the big guy from the house. He drew a knife and walked towards Caz. She was calm now, just stared at him without fear.

"My employer wants me to let you live, but he wants me to cut your face, very cruel, but that's what he wants."

He moved towards her again; she didn't take one step back.

"You can watch this Mr Carey, I'll finish you next."

This was very personal, payback for the aggravation we had been causing, I felt for my knife in my belt, just one chance, that's all I needed.

He lunged, not seriously but toying, he had caught her because I could see blood.

She let out a scream and took a step back drawing the gun. Good girl was all John could think, please, please shoot him.

It was only a small calibre but if she hit him he would go down, I would make sure I got to him with my knife, and he would never get up.

He stood there and laughed, then there was silence; it seemed to go on and on.

"My dear girl," he said, "it takes a certain kind of person to shoot a man in cold blood like this, and I'm sure that person is not you."You could have cut the silence with a knife, it seemed to go on for ever. He started to move in.

"YOU MEAN SOMEONE LIKE ME?"

John looked towards the voice. It was a large man about fifty, in a white shirt, MEEKS. Number five paused for a moment. "And you are?"

"Meeks, remember me?"

Number five started to turn slowly to face the voice. I knew he had a gun under his coat, but I never had time to shout and he never had time to draw it. Mr Meeks shot him straight between the eyes, without a flicker of emotion.

"Remember me now?""Welcome to the company, Mr Meeks," John said. "God I hope you've got good medical insurance, that's for sure."

John liked this man straight away.

Caz was by his side trying to see the extent of his wounds. I could see she had a gash to the top of her arm and it had caught her cheek but she would be fine. I let her fuss over me because it kept her busy and stopped her thinking about what had just happened.

"Meeks," I called. He came over. "Thanks mate, it was getting rough there for a while."

"Not a problem, the best I've felt in years." And looking at his face I could see he meant it.

"Did you know he had a gun?" I asked.

"I didn't think about it, I fully intended killing him from the moment I walked in the door."

"That's what I thought, you'd better phone Charlie Densil, tell him what has happened here, tell him that if he needs help from the spooks I can arrange it, that should stir him up.""Then wipe that gun and give it to Caz. You put your fingerprints all over it Caz, YOU, shot him

Caz, right?"

Meeks was just about to protest.

"You have a history with this lot, you were sacked for attacking one of them, they will slaughter you especially if it goes to court, they won't even question Caz, they cut her and shot me, it's self defence, you know I'm right."

"OK," he said grudgingly, wiping the gun and giving it to Caz.

"It's not your gun, is it?" I said slightly alarmed.

"No, no, it belongs to number six who was on lookout," answered Bill.

"What a shame we couldn't get one alive, we need people to testify against his bloody lordship."

Bill smiled at me. "Oh he's alive all right, all tied up in the shed, he's got a few lumps, but he wouldn't come quietly."

"Bill, I could kiss you." This man was going to fit right in. He was talking to Charlie Densil on the phone, so I don't think he heard.

Caz was crying just a little, John put his hand on her arm. "It's over now Caz, we are alive, we won."

"It's not that John, it's just that I got you shot. I didn't stay upstairs, I turned on that bloody light and I couldn't shoot that bastard. Talk about a feeble woman."

"Look Caz, you have just been stabbed, yet you are here dressing my wounds. Most people, male or female, would be in bits after what you just went through, also you faced that killer down, you looked him in the eyes and stood your ground. It unnerved him, believe me, that was why he made that silly wave with the knife, he was unsure. This enabled Bill the few seconds he needed to get in position.

"If he had done what he came for instead of trying to frighten you, Bill would have had to shoot him from the door, the bullet could have gone straight through him and into you, so you did more than most people could dream of.

As for getting me shot, YES you did and I will never let you forget it. EVER!"

She sobbed, "John, I love you," and took him in her arms. There was a slight smile on John's lips.

"All right, all right,' said Bill, "the law will be here any minute."

I'm sure he wiped his eyes.

Just then it all started happening. Charlie Densil walked in.

"Fucking hell, you didn't say it was the BLOODY ALAMO, sorry miss, didn't see you there.'"

Caz smiled.

"Inspector Charles Densil meet Mrs Caroline Hollins."

It was probably the last thing I got to say before the paramedics were all over me and I was prepared for whisking off to hospital.

I do remember hearing Caz saying, "Nice to meet you Charlie, I've heard a lot about you."

"Likewise miss er. Mrs." I couldn't see but I would bet big Charlie was blushing.

"Your old man's not going to like this one little bit," he said regaining his composure.

"We won't tell him for a few days, until he's back." Caz realised she had said too much.

"Back?" said Charlie, he didn't miss a thing.

"He's just away for a couple of days," said Caz unconvincingly, confirming to the inspector she had let slip more than she had meant to.

"Look my love, I've a pretty good idea what he's up to, I already know about the plane that didn't arrive in Italy and had a fictitious pilot, I will stick my neck out as far as I can to help, just you remember that. Here's my private mobile number, if he needs help call, any time, right? Now you two

114

get to hospital."

"Oh Charlie I love you too." She put her arms around his neck and kissed his cheek.

"Come on, get these people out of here, now," said the inspector, completely thrown by this show of affection.

Just then Sergeant Millar carried in the man from the shed. "Look what I found in the shed.""Oh yes," chipped in Bill Meeks, "I forgot about him, he was their lookout."

Sergeant Millar stood him up. He looked about him, absorbing the carnage in front of him, scarcely able to believe his eyes.

"L ... look I'm just a driver, the usual one's in hospital."

Bill Meeks put an arm round his shoulder, pulled him aside and whispered in confidence, "Look old son, you are going to tell the inspector everything and I mean everything, and then I might keep quiet about the gun, which just happens to have killed someone in here, also belongs to you and has your fingerprints all over it. Just one more thing, the normal driver you spoke of is dead, killed by your boss, so this is your last chance believe me. Don't speak just think before you say anything."

The poor man realised he was in serious trouble, but he wasn't stupid. It didn't take long for him to understand that his only chance was to talk, and he would.

"OK, I'll tell you what I can, but you'll have to look after me."

"Sergeant. Take him away and have a good chat," said the normally enigmatic inspector.

You could see the excitement on his face no matter how emotionless he tried to look. He could feel the evidence growing all the time. He would still keep pushing all the time now, until he won or became unemployed trying.

CHAPTER FIFTEEN (MAGGIE)

I awoke to a lovely sunrise over the mountains, the temperature in my little tent had become uncomfortable which had caused me to wake early. I sat back and enjoyed the remainder of my bread and meats washed down with water. Sitting there with this beautiful view spreadeagled in front of me, it was easy to forget why I was there and what could lie ahead.

I packed up and cleared the site as well as I could. I took a lingering look over the site; I decided that it was as clear as I could make it.

If someone was searching for me, I don't think they would spot anything, which was the reason I never had a fire. In these mountains, a good tracker could smell a fire for miles, long before he could see the smoke, Let's hope their trackers weren't that quality. I set off on the last leg to Maggie.

"Well here we go Davey."

"Please Sarah, don't call me Davey."

"Sorry sweetie."

"Or bloody sweetie!" I snapped.

"I'm sorry David, I'm bloody jumpy as well you know." She sounded very subdued.

"Look darling," I said, 'I'm sorry, I didn't mean to snap, shall we go and get her then?"

"That's fine, but I don't think you should call me darling, you naughty boy, you could turn a girl's head!" We set off, I mean I set off, she wasn't doing any walking obviously; I don't know what she was doing, hovering I suppose. It took us about four hours to reach Grazalema. I walked up a gentle slope approaching the village. I'd never approached from this direction before and if possible it was even more beautiful from this view. Whatever, it was certainly an iconic Spanish mountain village, but I wasn't here for the view. I now entered the outskirts of the village, little cobbled streets with shuttered windows on little dark houses.

"There's a man hiding in the second doorway. He looks like he's waiting for you." It was Sarah.

"Is he armed?" I asked.

"I don't think so, he doesn't look like a killer just a bit shifty."

I thought I knew who it was, but still had to be careful. As I approached the doorway I drew my pistol, I swung into the doorway with my pistol out in front.

"Fucking hell Manus. It's me, you daft prick, who the bloody hell are you, James bloody Bond?"

It was Stan.

"How did you know I was bloody there?"

He was a bit shaken by having a gun shoved in his face, so I gave him a few seconds and said, "How are you mate? Nice to see you."

"I'm OK, you still haven't told me how you knew I was there."

I couldn't tell him the truth. "Someone told me there was a shifty character hiding in the doorway, so I knew it was you but had to be sure."

He didn't believe a word but had decided to ignore me and carry on.

"They are on to you mate, whoever they are, they came to the house and they knew you had emailed. I told them you had, but you did regularly, they seem to believe me.

I think if I had denied it they would have been on me like

a ton of bricks.

They asked me if you flew, I said that you usually drove, but they kept on about flying. I told them that you had flown but normally you drove." "Where did you land?""I told them Malaga and you once landed at a private strip and that loads of farmers had little strips for crop dusting and I had no idea which one you might have used.""I've no idea if they crop dust here but they didn't question it, and that's all I can tell you Manus."

"OK Stan, thanks, I'd better get to Los Narangos, the restaurant, the sooner I talk to her the sooner I can get out of here. I bet they can't be far behind us."

"Leave your bag with me, I'll refill it with food and drink and I can leave it here. You can pick it up on the way out."

"Cheers Stan, I'll get going. You just keep your head down and leave this bit to me."

"Don't you worry about me, I'll keep out of sight. And good luck."

I moved off as quickly as I could, crossed the Plaza De Espana, took a seat under an orange tree towards the front of the restaurant and waited. I didn't have to wait long before I saw her. She was the double of her mother, younger of course, but I would have known her without any problem.

I heard a gasp. "Isn't she beautiful?" said a proud mother. "She's like her mother, as you well know," I said, gesturing to Maggie that I needed attention. She made her way to me with a broad smile.

"Can I help you sir?"

"My name is David, you've been told to expect me, is that not true?"

"Some man told me you would be coming to take me away, but I'm not in the habit of going off with strangers just like that, especially in secret."

"Listen sweetie!" This was Sarah speaking. I would never call anyone sweetie!

"We haven't time to argue, there are some bad people getting very close to me and you, they could be here any moment, and if they do it is too late, they will kill us."

"Why should I trust you? Where's Mum, why is she not here?"I could see she was close to tears, she was worried sick about her mum, she didn't know who to trust, I felt like cuddling her.

"Ask her if there is one thing that I know that nobody else could possibly know unless I'd told them."

I still had this overwhelming feeling like I was her dad and wanted to make everything better for her.

But I had to concentrate on convincing her that I was on the level.

"Listen Maggie, is there anything that Mum knows that nobody else could know unless you or your mum had told them?"

"Just say to her, Tinkerbell."

I took her hands in mine, looked her in the eyes, took a deep breath and said,

"What about Tinkerbell?" She was visibly shocked, she turned bright pink and mumbled, "Hh how did you ... OK I'll come, but tell me where Mum is and what's happened."

"Look, I'll make a deal with you, we leave now, but as soon as we're clear, I'll tell you everything, but there is a condition, when I've told you, then you tell me about Tinkerbell!"

At least she smiled, I think she was beginning to trust me a bit, or at least not to feel so threatened by me.

"OK, I'll get my bag," she said relaxing now she'd made the decision. "Meet me over there in the alley, just so we are not seen leaving here together."And I was up and away before she had time to worry.

She arrived within minutes and we made our way through the narrow streets, heading for the hills but trying not to be seen. I was getting very uneasy and was desperate to be in my plane on our way home. The bag was where Stan had said, I grabbed it and rapidly moved to the track which would take us clear of the village. I knew that for the first few kilometres we could be seen from the village. Should somebody take the time to scan the hills with binoculars, we could easily be spotted, it would give whoever was looking not only our position but where we were heading.

In fact the game would be up for us, so until we were clear of the ridge and out of sight I remained on edge. The ground we needed to cover was fairly easy going so we made good progress. I figured after about twenty minutes we were out of sight from the village, and on a nice gentle slope back to my plane. Little did I know that within minutes of us leaving, a large black car arrived in the village, four men alighted and started looking. It was me they were looking for, they had photos and were asking everyone if they recognised me. Typical of the Spanish and their reluctance to be of help to any form of authority, they all shook their heads.

"*El hombre la chica ingles?*" A universal puzzled look.

"No *señor.*"

Friends who live and love Spain tell me this dislike for authority, in this region is a legacy from the civil war, at least it was working in our benefit that day. Fortunately it never occurred to them to scan the hills for the fugitives.

"Slow down a bit David, she's struggling."

I took a look, she was managing fine.

"Sarah," I said. I was developing a technique of talking with Sarah without actually talking out loud, which had stopped people from thinking that I'd lost my mind completely.

"Will you shut up, she's fine, in fact she's managing better than most would. While we are talking, why am I getting all these parental emotions for her? I'm not her dad."

"Look I'm sorry," she answered.

"When you got all the information from me, I suppose you got some of the emotional stuff along with it, what can I do?"

It made sense, I was feeling all paternal towards her, something I had not a clue how to handle.

We carried on walking for about two hours with Sarah in my ears continually singing Maggie's praises. I think it was just nerves.

"Shall we stop for a bite to eat now?" I said. **"OK,"** she answered.

We sat in silence for a few minutes, even Sarah. I knew what was coming and was not looking forward to it one little bit.

"My mum's dead, isn't she?"

I waited for a few seconds.

"Yes Maggie, she is."

She collapsed in tears, sobbing uncontrollably, her body shaking. I just held her and let her cry out as much as possible, even Sarah had gone quiet.

CHAPTER SIXTEEN (THE SHEPHERD)

She calmed down after a while, although she still looked completely devastated and was still sobbing occasionally, dry sobs like a child.

I had no choice now but to tell her everything. She already had her worst fears confirmed, so I could see no good reason to keep anything till later, so I took her hand and told her everything, from her mum's murder, right up to how I arrived here. She was quiet now, analysing what she had been told.

"Right, Mum was killed by Lord what's his name, who was also her stepson?"

"He didn't actually do the deed, but he ordered it, yes," I answered to her question.

"So who actually drove the car?" she asked.

"A man called Mark Thompson, a hired killer, who has since been murdered himself, on the orders of your half-brother. Well, we are pretty sure."

"The next thing I don't understand," she continued, "even if I inherit a major shareholding, as I understand it we are talking millions, so why kill everybody, surely there is more than enough to go round?"

"Well sweetie." There's Sarah again, but I carried on. "Firstly we are talking billions, the corporation, YOUR corporation to be accurate, is amongst the largest in the world, certainly one of the largest privately owned. As to why? I can only wonder myself. You are of course right, there is more than enough to go round, but he seems to have lost all rationality and is on a killing spree that must be stopped.

This all seems to go back to when your mother left and has been getting worse. It's difficult to know what he might do next."

"And Mother talks to you? Is she here now?"

"Sarah," I spoke out loud. There was silence. "You don't seem to query the fact that she talks to me.""I'm not at all surprised if I'm honest. Mum has always done things other people wouldn't even imagine, so I'm not that surprised."

"I can well believe that, Maggie my dear."

"You two can stop ganging up on me, right now." Sarah was back.

"Your mum says we are ganging up on her."

"Ask her why she can't talk to me," said Maggie.

"I don't bloody know, that's just how it is, I'm a newcomer to all this as well," snapped Sarah.

I passed it on to Maggie. The three-way conversation carried on for a while, it seemed to help Maggie in as much as she felt in truth she still had her mum, well to a degree.

I'd had enough of being go-between. It was more than a man could take, so I said I had to check my messages. It was in fact true, I was somewhat later than I should have been, so I moved aside, got my phone out and started to check. What I read was like a bullet in my chest.

House attacked by gunmen, I've a couple of stitches but am FINE, John been shot three times but is also OK. Bill Meeks saved me, five gunmen dead, one prisoner who is singing, please don't worry. I could go home but don't want to leave John. LOL miss you CAZXXX

PS we won! DON'T WORRY!!!!

I just sat staring into space, trying to come to terms with how close I'd come to losing the one thing that made sense of my life. What would I have done if I had lost her? I was finding it hard to have a cogent thought, I felt close to losing it.

"What's up David?" asked Maggie.

I showed her my phone. "Oh my god, I'm so sorry."

"It's not your fault," I answered.

"It's my relative, I feel responsible," she said. "He could have kept it all, if it saved one life, I'd have willingly let him have the lot."

"Sweetie, you're missing the point, he never asked you, he just decided, anyone who was or might be in his way, had to die. He doesn't think like you and me, he's a psychopath or whatever name they put on it these days."

We got ourselves together and moved off. We kept a good pace now all sloping downhill, we travelled in complete silence, both lost in our own thoughts and both knowing we neither wanted nor needed anybody intruding on this process, just time to sort out our own demons. Even Sarah had been silent for some time.

It had reached the time when we would have to stop for the night, I put up the tent for Maggie and we sat down to eat the last of our food, but we should be at Paco's by mid morning and we would never be allowed to leave without a massive hot meal.

"David."

"Yes I can hear." I'd heard someone on the path. "Do you know who it is? I think it is only one."

She was silent for a few seconds. "I think it's a shepherd, he's on his own, well just a few sheep or goats, he's armed." There was nothing sinister about that, most of these men that work in the mountains carry guns. He now came into view, about two hundred metres down the track, he looked like a typical goatherd or shepherd. Large, sturdy boots, the lower half of his trousers strapped with what I would describe as gaiters – scorpions and snakes were plentiful in these mountains – and of course the customary flat cap.

The one thing which did make me take note, he was carrying his gun over his back, which the locals all did, but it was a rifle not a shotgun, the usual weapon of choice among local mountain men.

He had seen us now and gave a wave. I eased my pistol to where it was easily accessible, the hairs on the back of my neck were standing up, my whole body was on alert, but I wasn't sure why.

I thought perhaps the message had fired me up so much I was itching to find someone to kill. I knew there was an element of truth to this, since getting the message, the whole killing, hunting, ruthless persona of former years was back. I needed to control it! He was getting close now, he was smiling. "*Buenos dias mi amigo*, Paco asked me to look out for you and bring you in."

I heard Sarah's voice. **"David."**

"I know," I answered without speaking, "I've seen."

She was drawing attention to the rifle, now I could see it close up I could see it was Paco's, the sniper rifle I had given him all those years ago in Italy. There was no mistake, Paco had made two little brass plates, one for each side of the stock, the one I could see said, *EL HERMANO*, my brother. I knew on the other side of the stock would be the one that read, GOD'S AVENGING ARM.

I knew that Paco would never give that rifle to anyone willingly, so either this guy took it, or Paco let him take it, knowing I would spot it and be warned.

"*Ola*," I said and gave him a glass of wine.

"How is Paco? And who are you?"

"He said you would be suspicious. I am his cousin Nino, I've come to stay for a while."

I was sure he was lying but I couldn't do anything while he was holding the rifle. One shot from that would kill whoever it hit, and should you be in line it would go straight through and kill you as well.

I bent down to get him some food. Maggie was still in the tent. I managed to whisper, "Don't show yourself, cut the back and get out if you can, try and hide in the rocks, don't let him see you, stay hidden until I call you."

She didn't answer, I just hoped she'd heard.

I took the food to Nino and sat down next to him, and tried to keep his attention away from the tent. I kept plying him wine hoping it would slow him down somewhat when the time came. I must admit it didn't seem to make much difference. I hadn't noticed any movement round the tent.

"Sarah, Sarah." "Oh I thought you were having a party with your new friend," she snapped.

"Look, you stupid cow, has Maggie got away from the tent, can you check?"

"Hang on," she said, getting the message this was serious.

A few seconds went by.

"Yes she's gone, I don't know where but there's no sign of her."

"Great."

I could now try and see to our friend. I took my pistol out and put it on the ground, I could see him visibly relax. He now was convinced that I trusted him. The real reason being if I fired my pistol, it would be heard at Paco's, they would know the difference between my pistol and the rifle, so I was pretty sure they would come charging up to the rescue. I had no idea how many they were and wanted to look before having to fight.

I reached down and unclipped the sheath round my knife so it would be ready.

"Have you got the girl, *señor*?"

"She's gone up in the hills for a wash, you know, a bit of

privacy."

"*Si*," he nodded. I don't know whether he believed me or not but he seemed relaxed, the light was fading fast now.

"More wine?" I asked.

"*Si*," he said.

I made as if to get up and get the wine, I staggered, feigning drunkenness. I lay on the floor giggling, hoping he was convinced.

"You'll haf to gedit," I said snorting and laughing.

He moved off his rock still holding the rifle, then he propped it up against a rock out of my reach. He obviously thought I would be after the rifle, when all I wanted was to separate him from it. He got the wine from the bag and started to move back. I was pretending to try and stand, as he drew close to me I slipped the knife from its sheath, put my hand on him supposedly to steady myself. I drew back the knife and plunged it into his thigh. He let out a scream and lunged for the rifle. But my blood was up now, I couldn't do anything to the people that hurt my wife, but this beauty was just about to kill both me and a teenage girl who I loved like a daughter. I grabbed him by his hair and dragged him away from the rifle, lifted him up onto his feet, stuck the knife in his back, just enough so that the blade penetrated his skin by about an inch, so he got the message.

"No *señor*, please they made me do it."

"Paco and his family, are they still alive?"

"*Si, Si*, they are unhurt."I spun him round and punched him full force on the nose which erupted into a bloody mass. His nose was broken, he'd lost teeth, he now realised that he was dealing with a violent man who didn't know the meaning of mercy, and he was frightened.

"Look Nino my friend, if I once even think you're not telling me the truth, I shall fillet you with this knife. It will take you a long while to die, do you understand?"

"*Si.*"

"How many are at the farm?"

"*Dos*, truly *señor.*"

"Have they damaged the plane?"

"No, the two there are going to kill everyone, make it look like you did it, and keep the plane for themselves."I thought he was telling the truth, I couldn't be sure but it sounded right. Two at the farm, this one three, maybe three more at Grazalema, they wouldn't have more, it would start to be noticed by the locals and it would attract attention.

"You were supposed to kill us and throw us off the mountain, yes?"

"*Si.*"

"Well that seems like a good idea, it would be months before anyone found you up here."

I gave him an almighty shove. He realised it was over, there was a look of resignation on his face as he flew over the edge and screamed all the way down.

I made sure the bandolero holding the ammunition for the rifle was left behind, I was going to need it.

I noticed Maggie, leaning against the rocks, her face completely without colour, all I could see was shock.

I realised that she must have witnessed what had just occurred. She realised that she didn't know or understand this man that she had began to trust and look to for support, and had seemingly shown himself as a cold-blooded killer.

"Maggie," I said and held out my hand. I had to try and sort this out now otherwise she may never trust me.

"Come here, sit down and listen."

She moved to me, hesitantly, but took my hand and sat down.

"Be careful, she's on the edge." It was Sarah. "She's not a

tough old bird like her mum."

"Listen, just let me talk, don't interrupt, we need to get this out of the way. Now what you just witnessed shocked you, yes?"

"Yes, is that surprising?"

"No of course not, but I want you to look at it from my point of view. I've got this young girl, sorry, young woman, who has been suddenly thrust upon me."

I could see the hurt straight away in her eyes.

"Wait, this young woman who I've only just met, and yet I have all these feelings for her, feelings I don't understand.

I can rationalise all this, because I think when your mum transferred all that information into me, she never had time or the energy to filter bits she wanted transferred and the bits she didn't, so I got the lot, including the way she feels. So I got the lot, including the way she feels. So now I feel all this love for you, all these paternal feelings, do you understand what I mean?"

"I think so, but ..."

"The shepherd, right."

She nodded.

"Well firstly he was not a shepherd, he was a killer, sent to kill us, he may have already killed my friends and their family. He was going to throw you off the mountain, then he would take me to my friend's farm, kill all of them, if he hasn't already, and make it look like I was responsible."

She had a look of anger beginning to emerge on her face. She wanted to believe what I told her, but my cold-blooded dealing with Nino was a worry to her.

"Look, you know I'm an ex-soldier?"

She nodded.

"Well when someone I care about is threatened I react like a soldier. I will eliminate them, whether that means you or other people I love are upset or see me in a different way, then I can live with that. My job is to see you survive and make sure you live long enough to decide whether I was wrong or right.

The thing is I don't know for sure, but I only know one way to react, which I do and hope I'm right. I'm finding it hard as well, I'm not the twenty-one-year-old with not a doubt about anything,

I'm older with a different life, but I force myself to do things because I know it's right, but it's not easy."

She looked at me long and hard then put her arms around my neck and said, "Mum chose you and I think she did OK."

"Thanks sweetie, sorry that's your mum's words again." "I know, I'm beginning to get the hang of this now!""We'd better get what sleep we can and move out first thing.

Can you keep watch, Sarah?"

All was quiet, then, "**Don't I get to sleep then**?"

"You don't sleep, you're a spirit, aren't you? Not physical, therefore you don't need rest."

"How come you know so bloody much about it all of a sudden?" Then she mumbled and I heard, **"Just go to bloody sleep and leave it all to me."**

CHAPTER SEVENTEEN
(GOD'S AVENGING ARM)

A few hours of fitful sleep was all we managed, the adrenaline coupled with the knowledge of what was to come, fired our bodies and kept us feeling good. We were on the hills overlooking Paco's farm by first light. I took up a vantage point with a good view of all the buildings and waited. I kept searching with my binoculars, but as yet had not spotted a soul. Whether this was good or bad I had no way of knowing, but I knew I needed to know who was there before I could plan.

"Have you seen anyone?" It was Maggie.

"Not as yet but we will, I just hope it's Paco and his family."And so we continued to wait, the sun was getting higher now and beginning to warm pleasantly.

"There, look," said Maggie, pointing to one of the outbuildings. Two men were walking from the house to the main outbuilding, which I hoped still housed the plane. From this distance I couldn't recognise who they were, even with the binoculars, all I could do was watch and wait.

They entered the outbuilding and were lost from view.

"Sarah."

"Yes," she replied.

"Is there a chance you could go down and see what's happening? If they're alive? Anything that can help me."

"I'll try."

And then I suppose she was gone. I can't always tell what she's up to but several time she has given us the edge, let's hope she can now.

The two men came out of the barn. They were holding a third man at rifle point, which I surmised must be Paco. I raised the rifle to my shoulder, I had them both in the open with nowhere to hide, would I ever get a better chance. There was as far as we knew only two of them, and they were both in front of me. I took aim, but hesitated, something did not feel right, what was it? I'd been a soldier long enough to take notice of these feelings, but having them at my mercy! I raised the sight to my eye.

"Don't shoot, don't shoot!" It was Sarah. **"The man with the gun is Paco, the man in the blue jacket is the bad guy."**

Suddenly I could understand why I felt something was wrong. I knew I recognised the man with the rifle, Paco, just by the way he stood. It was enough to make me delay and think, he was holding the rifle left handed. Paco was right, but on the butt I could see a carving. I couldn't read it from this distance but I knew what it was instinctively. He had carved, GOD'S AVENGING ARM.

I had seen this but it didn't register until now. He was trying to warn me in the only way he could think of. I was still looking through my binoculars, I couldn't make out details but everything was clear to me now. I raised the rifle sight to my eye, cold this time, no emotion, I knew what had to be done. Mr blue coat was in my sight, I moved the crosshairs up to his head.

"Be ready Paco," I mumbled to myself. I started to squeeze.

WOOMF.

I fired. This gun was extremely quiet for the power it created, and with a very manageable kick.

Mr blue coat hit the floor, minus, astonishingly, his head. I did wonder momentarily what one of the exploding shells

132

would be capable of. Paco and Carlos hit the floor and started to crawl to shelter. There was quite a distance to go so I would probably need to be in action again.

The door to the main building crashed open and killer number two came rushing through. I'll never understand why he would expose himself like that to try and kill two unarmed men who were shackled together, inevitably bringing himself under my fire. I was his biggest problem, not Paco and Carlos but he seemed oblivious to this. He would never have time to consider his mistake as he was still moving forward as my sights moved on to him. I never had time to take careful aim, speed was utmost in my mind. WOOMF, another head departed this world.

"Fuck." Maggie was right next to me.

"Well miss," I said, surprised to hear her swear.

"Oops, sorry, but my god that gun, that must be four to five hundred metres."

I thought about explaining that it was the man operating the gun, but thought better of it. I still kept a close eye on the sight until I was sure there was no more danger. I saw Maria come through the door of the main building and run towards Paco and Carlos. They had started to get to their feet, Paco just had time to look up towards where he knew I would be and give me a wave before Maria grabbed him round the neck and show the relief she felt to have her family safe.

Maggie sat next to me and was wiping a tear. Was it because they were all safe, or was it because she could see the family she had missed out on? I put my arm around her shoulder and helped her up. One thing had changed, she wasn't worried about the two killers I'd shot.

"We had better get down there and I'll introduce you to them, then you'll really know why I had to save them."

"Whatever you do, don't thank me, I'm just a bloody corpse." It was Sarah.

"Listen Lady Sarah, thank you for stopping me shooting, I think I was just about to fire when you shouted, and not for the first time, you have been the only reason that we are not just surviving. But I think you give us a chance of winning."

Silence.

I did glance at the rifle, what a weapon, I'd got this one as an experimental version years ago, just to test. I'm not even sure if it's in production as yet, being out of the forces for some time, but this weapon is terrific, to think it was made by a small English firm in Portsmouth.

I must talk to them should I survive just to say thanks.

CHAPTER EIGHTEEN (MIKE)

Mike drove to work in a bit of a daze. He could not stop thinking about Sammie, he knew how he felt about her, although he couldn't get past the feeling that it was wrong to try and replace his best friend in her affections. Common sense told him that was stupid but it didn't stop the feelings that he couldn't shake off.

He was pleased that she wasn't involved in the present situation, and thought perhaps if he could get revenge he might change his ideas. He had thought non-stop about this since his talk with David and felt there was a real chance that his dreams of revenge were now a real possibility.

He pulled into his parking spot, stopped his dreaming and got his head straight, ready for work.

He walked into the foyer after using his ID card. Both guards were already in place, he said his good mornings, wondering if they slept in those positions all night. He couldn't help considering how pleased he was that they were on our side, he certainly wouldn't want to try and go up against them. They were a formidable looking pair that was for sure. He sat in his office, went through all the stories, they had been sorted into groups, made some phone calls then faxed them to various papers. Just a normal day earning the money to pay the wages.

He would then get back to Lord Benson. He had continued to feed the papers with little titbits of information and the broadsheets with the more heavy financial scandals.

It was working as well. The share prices were diving, the papers were full of rumours about Lord B. It had not been difficult, the man had so many enemies, the phone was constantly ringing, people queuing up to tell things they had heard but were too frightened to repeat.

It should be a lesson for anyone in business. If at all possible, don't make enemies, the grudge festers forever. Then should the chance present itself where they can gain revenge, they fall over themselves to plunge the knife in, the deeper the better.

Friends on the other hand gather round to help and cover you wherever they can.

But these people's egos would never allow them to consider that they can't bully everybody to their will, and they often live to regret it. The phone shocked him from this philosophical train of thought.

"Hello." It was Mary.

"I thought you would want to take this call."

He lifted the handpiece. "OK, can I help?"

"Is that Michael Denby?"

"Yes speaking, who's this?"

"This is Holloway Hospital, we have a Mrs Samantha Carey. I'm sorry to tell you that she's been involved in an RTA. We have her in A&E. She appears to be quite badly hurt. Hello, hello?"

The phone was hanging from the desk, the office door swinging, Mike had gone. The lift door opened, Mike ran to the front door and straight past both guards. They tried to talk to him but he was not stopping for anything, they watched him run to his car.

Mary came out of the lift. "Where has he gone?" she gasped.

One of the guards grabbed her.

"What happened?"

"He had a phone call from the hospital and rushed off.

It was the Holloway, about Sammie."

The guard let her go and looked out of the door just to see Mike pulling out of the car park.

"Right, phone the hospital, find out if the call was genuine and let me know." With that he took off out of the door. We all stood watching him fly down the road like an Olympic sprinter.

"PHONE!" shouted the other guard.

Mary grabbed the nearest phone and was in full action. She had realised the problem that could be imminent if the call was false. She was talking forcefully to someone at the hospital already.

"Are you sure? Could you check one more time?"

She covered the mouthpiece. "It appears no one seems to have heard of Samantha Carey."

She put the phone to her ear. "Yes, and that's certain, OK thank you very much." She said goodbye and put the phone down.

"It appears the call was false."

The second guard had his phone to his ear already waiting for number one to answer. "Jim, the call was phony so expect trouble, right?"

"What chance has he got?" said Mary.

"He's on foot and Mike's in a car for Christ's sake."

"Listen all of you, how far is the hospital? A couple of miles maybe a bit more?"

We all nodded. It was just along the Fulham road.

"Well there will only be seconds in it, in fact Jim has a good chance of getting there first, believe me."

"He has no traffic lights or roundabouts to worry about, he can do two miles in ten minutes with ease."

We all felt better because we knew it took ten to fifteen minutes in a car, so we could hope.

Mike pulled into the hospital, screeched to a halt, jumped from the car and started sprinting to A&E.

He should have heard the motorbike roar into the car park after him, but was not seeing or hearing anything around him, just focusing completely on Sammie and his own blind panic. He heard nothing but he did feel a sharp burning in his leg and was falling although he had no idea why. He looked up and saw the gunman standing astride his motorcycle with what he immediately realised was a gun.

He knew straight away that he'd been set up. He did have doubts while driving here, but now he was just so angry with himself, what a bloody idiot.

He started to rise and try to stand, his leg didn't seem too painful which surprised him somewhat. He still wasn't thinking right, just presenting the gunman with a bigger target. He saw the gunman raise his gun and take careful aim, he had his victim at his mercy, he felt no need to rush.

Mike closed his eyes and waited for what he felt was coming. He felt himself lifted bodily from the ground and shoved into the wall and onto the ground. He opened his eyes to see Jim the guard standing in front of him, raising a pistol himself. The next few seconds were like being in a war zone, a full fire fight. Then the silence which seemed to go on forever. It seemed like slow motion but was just seconds. Jim was leaning against the wall.

"Are you OK?" he said.

"To be honest I haven't a fucking clue, what about you?" was all he could manage to mumble.

Mike could see he was bleeding all over the place.

"I'm fine," he said which didn't surprise him "You stay there until help comes. Say nothing, just tell the police to talk to me."

"Where are you going? You're hurt."

"I'm going to make sure the gunman can't get away. I took care not to kill him so I don't want to waste all that effort.

Mike watched him stagger over to the motorbike. It appears the gunman had three bullets in his leg then one in the shoulder,

138

that was his gun arm, he would never walk properly on that leg but nothing life threatening.

People were all arriving, doctors, nurses and sirens were everywhere in the car park. Within minutes there were police everywhere. He noticed Jim the guard showing them a warrant card of some sort and the police seemed to almost bow. There was definitely some sort of deference to him because of this card. I wondered just who he was? He was beginning to become somewhat dizzy, as a doctor and several nurses arrived and started to work on him. It appears, as he subsequently found, that a bullet had managed to get past Jim, hitting him high on the left side of his chest, causing damage which needed an immediate session in the operating theatre. At that moment he blacked out, his last thought being, "I bloody hope I come round."

He next remembers looking up at the ceiling above my bed, he knew exactly where he was and what had happened, none of this where am I malarky.

"Mike." He heard her voice.

"Mike, are you awake?" He turned so he could see her, she was crying.

"Listen," he said,

"I bloody love you, I could have died out there without telling you, how fucking stupid is that?"

"Oh Mike, I thought you'd never open your mouth."

Then she kissed him.

He knew at that moment he would not die, in fact everything seemed to be working out rather well! Anyway, during his time in hospital they talked endlessly, which ended in him proposing, which of course surprised nobody. It seems that everybody knew our feelings all along. We spoke a lot about Sean and Jake, all our love and feelings for both of them which cleared all our worries, even for some unknown reason ended our mourning. He knew how he felt and nothing could stop that, even bullets.

CHAPTER NINETEEN (HOME)

We stood from the cover of the rocks and started to make our way down to the family. As we grew closer, they started to run towards us, we all clashed into a mass hug, Maggie was swept up in the emotion like a long-lost family member. I could see the tears streaming down her face, this family had just that same effect on me, always had, and it appears that Maggie was captivated by the same magic if her face was anything to judge by.

After a frantic few minutes it calmed down, so I made the introductions. Maria immediately took

Maggie in her arms.

"*Ahora estas asalvo querida,*" you're safe now sweetheart.

Maggie stood back still crying.

"B ... but it's me that put you in danger, because of me your whole family could have been killed, how can I ever make that up to you?"

Paco stepped forward holding up his arms, as a gesture for everyone to listen.

"This man here is, *el hermano* to my family. Unfortunately he has a knack of bringing trouble with him. I hoped he had grown out of it but, no, but we know absolutely in our hearts if he wants to help you, you are family as well, welcome to my family."

Maggie looked like she was about to faint. I'd underestimated what she'd been through over the last few days, and how it was getting to her. I reached forward to help her, but was beaten to it by Carlos, who swept her off towards the house with his arm around her.

"Are you watching them?" It was Sarah.

"Stop worrying and leave them alone, they have a lot in common. It'll do them good to talk."

"He's Latin!"

I couldn't help laughing.

"She's spent her whole life being Latin, what on earth are you thinking? And don't you dare eavesdrop, just leave them alone." She went quiet.

I could see them sitting out front of the house just talking. I thought it was just what she needed, probably both of them.

We had to have the obligatory family meal and celebration, which to be honest was a welcome relief from the tension we had been living. Well it was only a week or two but it had been so intense that nothing before that seemed to enter our thoughts. Halfway through the evening I noticed the two boys had disappeared. I sought out Paco, Phillipe and Carlos.

"*Amigo*, what are they about?"

He smiled.

"The gunmen, they will disappear and never be found."

I later found out that an old charcoal oven in the woods had been fired up and the two bodies were put in with the wood, when taken out, the fire had left just crumbling bones, not being hot enough to powder majority of the skeleton, which the boys hammered into tiny pieces and mixed with fertilisers to be spread round the farm. I think I could feel safe that they would never be found.

Morning came with a lovely Spanish sunrise, a slight heat haze over the tops of the mountains, beautiful sunshine and the promise of a warm day to come. It made me remember just how beautiful Spain was once you got away from the Costas. We had breakfasted early and I was now anxious to be on our way. The tension was back as I knew we were entering the climax of our story.

I had to get Maggie to a solicitor alive to sign and claim her inheritance.

Lord Nigel had to make sure, on the other hand, that somewhere between Spain and the solicitor, he or a hired gun killed her, simple really, as of course most things are. I was determined to keep Maggie alive, not for the money, but to have a long and happy life, she was like my daughter. Maybe because of Sarah and the feelings she passed onto me, maybe because she was just a sweet and nice girl. I knew that whatever or whoever tried to harm her, they would have to go through me and I wouldn't make it easy for them.

I started to try and get us to the plane, which was not going to be easy, what with the family yet again adopting a stray, and wanting us to stay and move in permanently. Experience had prepared me for this, so I just kept assuring them that as soon as we sorted things out we would be in touch.

Carlos was making some arrangements of his own, huddled together with Maggie talking with what looked like an intensity only they were privy to, which ended in a kiss. Whether it was for either of them their first kiss I had no way of knowing, but it seemed to have a profound effect on both of them that's for sure.

At last we managed to both get seated in the aircraft and started to prepare for take-off. I gave her a glance to see how she was bearing up. "Are you OK?" I said, a bit weak really but I wanted to make sure she was up for what was ahead.

"I'm fine, they are just so lovely, it makes you think about what you may have missed."

"You tell her I did my best, at least she's still alive." Sarah was feeling very hurt at what she obviously felt was criticism of her motherhood.

"Listen sweetheart, your mum did everything she could for you, she sacrificed her own life just to keep you alive.""I'm not blaming Mum for anything, far from it, and I don't feel that I missed out on anything, but we both missed out on things her and me, and then after all the sacrificing, they still killed her. All those years of worry and tension to keep me alive and they still managed to take the most precious thing in my life. She was everything to me and I never even got to tell her."

"You just did."

"You mean she's here? I can't feel her."

"She's here but she's just gone quiet, not for long I suspect."

We all went quiet, into our own thoughts, so I busied myself getting ready for take-off.

I fired the engines and found great comfort in the surge of power, happy with something I understood, a break from the emotional stuff that we men find difficult.

We surged forward, a final wave and we were airborne, climbing up and over the mountains, always a lovely feeling no matter how long you've been flying. I set a course for home and started to think about my plans to win the final encounter.

"Thank you, David." It was Sarah.

"For what?" I answered.

"You know what for, defending me, you knew I was hurt by what she said."

"I never said anything that wasn't true, did I?"

"Maybe not but it was nice to hear it, so thank you again." "You're talking to her, aren't you? Why don't you talk out loud? It's not fair."

"Sorry darling, but it was a bit personal, she did say that she wondered what she did right to make you such a wonderful, intelligent and gorgeous daughter."

"I must take after her," Maggie said with a smile.

"Yes," I answered, "she said that as well."

We both started to laugh.

"You always know the right words, don't you David?" said Sarah.

"Only when I care!" We flew on for about half an hour, time I thought to get started on our plan. I picked up the radio mouthpiece.

"Blackbushe this is bandit, Blackbushe this is bandit, do you copy over."A few minutes passed, I was just going to try again.

"You bastard, where have you bloody been? We've had the bloody law all over us, everyone thought you had crashed and it's not Jay is it? That's Dave!"

"Got me, you old bugger." I gave him the appropriate ID numbers.

"I'll be landing in about three hours. I'll tell you everything then, and Bill, no need to tell the law. I'll see them when I get back and square it all then, bandit out."

I was pretty sure that Bill would have the airport full of police within minutes of me going off air. Not that he was nasty but he just liked everything proper and right. I had mucked him about quite a bit without much explanation, so I was sure he would be on the phone already and would call an almighty commotion at Blackbushe which would suit me fine. I picked up my mobile and dialled Charlie Densil on his mobile.

"Hello Charlie?" A pause.

"Yes, this is Inspector Densil."

"It's David."

"Yes, what can I do for you?"

I guessed he was not alone.

"I'm on my way home and I need a favour."

"Yes and what's that?"

I was sure now by the tone of his voice that he did have people with him

"I've told everyone that I'm landing at Blackbushe and I'd like you to tell everybody there the same, especially the guy you think is passing stories on to Lord B.

Tell them we are going straight to my office to meet the solicitors. I am actually going to land at Popham. Do you know it? A little field on the A303 near Micheldever."

"Yes I know where you mean, are you bringing Mum's present?"

"Oh yes I've got it with me real close, but will need picking up, is that possible? Should be there about 11am, just you, I don't trust anyone else."

"Right, we are OK now, I'm alone," said Charlie.

"OK mate but you get the idea, I want them to be looking for us which should give us a bit of time, hopefully enough to get sorted."

"Dave, you can leave this to me, I see what you're planning, and I'll be with you. How's the present?"

"She's very special Charlie, you'll see when you meet her."

"Till then Dave."

"One more thing Charlie, could you come armed?"

"Not a problem, see you at eleven, and good luck." The line went dead.

"Was the present me?" asked Maggie.

"Yes it was," I answered. "I was talking to Inspector Charles Densil. He's a good friend of ours and is going to help."

"All these people that are willing to help without knowing me, I find it so hard to understand."

"Look sweetheart, it's the old good and evil thing, people recognise good, and they don't like bad, so they pick sides.

Always remember most people are pretty good on the whole, irrespective of what people might tell you, and I'm one that should know."

"I hope you're right David."

Then she went quiet, contemplating what had been happening to her I suppose. I leant down and picked up the mobile, the final part of the plan, god I hope I haven't forgotten anything.

"I tell you one thing I'm sure of," she said from her daze.

"What's that?" I responded.

"I'm not special!""You have no idea how special you are, but when this is all over, I'll sit you down and we'll discuss it, fair enough?"

She smiled.

"Fair enough."

"I still haven't been told about Tinkerbell!" She smiled and blushed.

I dialled Jimmy Charmicheal my favourite solicitor.

"Hello."

"Jimmy?"

"Yes, who's that?"

"David Hollins."

"Davey boy, where the bloody hell have you been?"

"Never mind all that, I've got a job for you, very important."

"Fire away." He was now in serious mode, so I launched into the details of what was needed from him.

"Right mate, I've got all that, leave it to me. I'll sort it and good luck."

"Right Jimmy and thanks," and he hung up.

Well hopefully everything was in place, all we had to do was to survive for the next few hours, that's all! We drifted into our own thoughts, a silence that lasted for well over an hour.

"What's up with you two?" Sarah was back again.

"We were just thinking, that's all."

"You're talking to Mum again, aren't you?" said Maggie.

I had perfected speaking with Sarah mentally only for Maggie to know straight away when it was occurring.

"Yes," I admitted.

"What did she say?"

"I told her we were just thinking, because she thought we were both quiet."

"Tell her I was wondering how I'm going to survive the next few hours, with a psychotic billionaire serial killer totally intent on my demise, after all he got you and you knew him and what he could do."

Sarah answered quietly,

"I didn't know he was capable of these sorts of things. His behaviour has completely changed since I knew anything of him, also you've got me and Mr Hollins, David looking after you. I was on my own, nobody to help me, feeling like you do now only for eighteen years."

I relayed Sarah's words, there was a long pause.

"Yes Mum, I don't know how you ever did it."

"Mother's love darling, mother's love, you'll know what I mean one day, believe me."

The tension was building up, we all knew what was at stake, to me I felt like I did when waiting to go into action. The difference being when you go into action you know the bad guys, they are in front of you, whereas now I'm not sure who they are or where they will come from. I have tried to outwit them but I would never underestimate Lord B.

You don't build a multinational company without being very astute intellectually and even allowing for the fact that he seems to have lost the plot somewhat and become, to say the least, psychotic. That intellect will be there somewhere.

It wouldn't be long now before we would be sighting the English coast then we would start dropping down. I must admit I wanted to land and get moving.

"There's the coast," called Maggie.

I looked up and there it was right in front of us and rapidly getting closer.

"It's only about half an hour or so until we land now."

Maggie nodded her head, she looked apprehensive which was to be expected. She was aware that she was the target and as much as she trusted me, it couldn't be easy to handle at her age, however amazing I knew she was.

"We won't take our bags, just a few things we need, I want to move fast when we land."

"OK." She wasn't about to start questioning my decisions at this time, I was grateful to her for that.

We were over the south coast and heading inland. I would leave it as late as possible before I spoke to the airfield, I didn't want to give them time to question anything or contact Blackbushe airport or anyone else come to that. I just wanted to get down and away, with the inspector's help, before anyone asked for papers or passports etc. and just disappear.

"How are you Maggie?"

She gave me a little smile.

"I'm fine Uncle Davey."

"Is she flirting?" Sarah was vocal again.

"Don't be silly, she picked up how worried I was and was trying to help."

I picked up the radio and called the tower at Popham. "Hello Popham, hello Popham this is bandit G—AEL Mayday Mayday, we are in trouble need to land, emergency, emergency."

"Say again please, this is Popham."

"Sorry no time, am coming in now, will see you when and if I get down OK?"

I was now in full view of the airfield, coming in low and fast over the A303 and dropping down to the runway, nobody could have had a good view of us, which was just how I wanted it.

"There is Inspector Densil, look in the Volvo to the left of the tower."

I spotted him then and thought, brilliant he had pulled up about four hundred metres from the small tower, which should give us time to get out and into the car before any officials can get to us and start asking for forms to be filled in and so on.

The wheels hit the runway hard, because of the speed I had come in, but the brakes were slowing us now as we got nearer to the inspector's car.

I stopped the plane as near as possible to the car and we were on our way in seconds. Maggie went first, grabbed by Charlie who ushered her into the back of the car. I followed seconds after. I paused for a quick look to see if we were in the clear, I could see there was one uniform getting close, we will just have to bluff.

"Here you are," said Charlie and passed me an automatic pistol. The engine roared into life and we started to move, it was then I realised that we had a driver I didn't recognise. I turned the pistol round to face him.

"Oh before you shoot him this is Bill Meeks, I thought we could do with the man power," said Charlie.

I held my hand out to him, he took it and shook it.

"I believe I owe you a big thank you."

"It was a great pleasure, sir."

"Thanks anyway, and never call me sir again!"

"Fair enough," he said and smiled.

"What's this guy think he's doing?" said the inspector. The uniformed airport security man had moved in front of us and was standing with his hand up instructing us to stop.

Bill Meeks pulled up with the inspector's door alongside the officer. He opened his window

"Where do you think you are going?"

The inspector showed his warrant card. "This is a very important police operation, I'm the senior officer, these people are all under my jurisdiction and it's imperative that we leave straight away."

"I'll need your names and proof of identity and then I'll decide if I will let you go or not, sir."

He moved to my position, having written down Charles' details. I gave him my passport and security card, given to me by John. I could see other people leaving the tower area, we would be swamped in minor officials in a few minutes.

'What regiment were you in officer?"

"3Para. Why?"

"Listen, as one soldier to another, I'm looking after this young lady because someone is trying to kill her. If I give my word that I will come back tomorrow and sort everything out with you, will you let us go now, please?"

He looked at Maggie. "Is that right miss?"

"Yes it's true."He thought for a minute.

"OK then and good luck. Oh by the way, what would you have done if I'd said no?"

I leaned back and showed him the pistol. "I'd have shot you."

He smiled. "That's what I figured, go on, see you tomorrow."

And off we went through the gate and down the 303 towards London.

CHAPTER TWENTY (A PLAN)

It seemed like in no time at all we were crossing the River Thames at Richmond.

"Just a few minutes now," I said. Why I don't know, they were all aware of where we were and where I lived, except Maggie of course, perhaps I said it just for her benefit. "Have you ever been to England before?" I asked her.

"Never, I suppose Mum was always worried about someone spotting us."

We drove through Mortlake and along the riverside at Barnes. The sun was glinting off the water, Victorian villas overlooking the river, many people rowing, a scene that has hardly changed in the last hundred years, and very English."Was that your first kiss?"

She looked quizzically at me.

"Carlos at the farm," I explained.

"Not the first, but the first that felt like that," she answered with a smile. We both laughed as we drove through the gates of my house.

Caz was waiting at the door as we climbed from the car. I noticed the bandage on her arm and the stitches on her cheek. I took her in my arms.

"How are you?"

"I'm fine, John's well on the mend, so is Mike, also Jim, one of John's gang. Oh of course you don't know anything about all this, let's go inside and I'll fill in the details."

She looked over my shoulder to where Maggie was standing.

"Oh I'm so sorry, this must be the one and only Maggie."

Maggie stepped forward. "Hello," she said, putting out her hand as if to shake hands.

"Oh Maggie," said Caz and took her in her arms. They cuddled for some time. As they broke apart, I heard Caz whisper, "You'll be all right darling, you belong to our family now and we'll look after you." Both looked on the brink of tears so I whisked them in through the door. Jimmy was already there.

"I never saw your car Jimmy."

"I parked at a pub about a mile away and got a cab, just in case somebody was looking for my car. It is a bit conspicuous, well some people think so."

"Good idea, shall we get on then?" I took them into my little office, sat Maggie down at the desk next to Jimmy.

"Now Jimmy will go through all the paperwork with you, both your father's will and your mother's will, then he will write your will. If there is anything you do not understand just stop him and ask him to explain, don't worry he's a pussy cat really, well when he's on your side that is anyway."

Maggie nodded.

She looked nervous but that was only to be expected. Eighteen and going through what she was having to cope with.

"Don't worry, I'll stay and keep an eye on him." She was back.

"Don't worry darling, Mum's watching." She looked at me and smiled, knowing exactly what I meant.

"That makes me feel much better."

I left them to it and joined the others who were tucking into large plates of food that Caz had prepared. I didn't realise how hungry I was, but was soon tucking in with Charlie and Bill.

"How's Maggie?" asked Caz.

"I've got to phone Sir Michael Perry, but I think she would appreciate you being with her."

"No problem." And she was gone.

I picked up my mobile just in case the home phone was bugged. I dialled Sir Michael's direct mobile number.

After a few rings I heard his familiar voice. "Hello David, what can I do for you?"

"Sir Michael."

I paused.

"The company we were discussing when we last spoke.""Mm yes I remember."

"Well I'm fairly certain that there will be a major change in the management/ownership structure of the whole group imminently."

"Good god!"

he exclaimed. "Is this definite or just a rumour?"

"I'm certain that baring a major catastrophe, it will happen."

I was reluctant to say more with the knowledge that there was a psycho killer still intent on stopping us.

"The reason I'm talking to you, Sir Michael, is that the new owner will need a CEO to run the group for her, and I thought of you."

There was a prolonged silence. "Well, it's very generous of you to think of me, especially considering why we first talked, but there are a few questions before we can proceed. Firstly, how can you possibly deliver this position?

You're not even a shareholder.

Secondly, I could in no way work with the present management, or run the company in the style it has been run. My style is hard but completely straight, there is no room for negotiation on this, these are the main concerns that spring to mind."

"That is perfect Sir Michael, and the very reason I would recommend you. As for delivering the post, please believe me should everything go to plan that would be no problem. To sum up, if you can be reassured on these points, you would be interested, yes?""Of course."

"Thank you Sir Michael, I should get back to you in the next twenty-four hours."

I finished the call, one more piece of the puzzle in place.

I made my way to the office to see how they were getting on. I took a tray of tea, coffee and food in case they were in need, judging by the reaction as I entered, I was right. They all helped themselves to food while I poured tea and coffee as required.

I sat down next to Jimmy. "How's it going?"

"Well she's a very bright girl, but I think she's going along with what I'm saying because you recommended me and she trusts you absolutely.""And I trust you absolutely Jimmy, so we should be fine." "I hope so mate."

"He seems very nice." It was Sarah. "I think he will do his best for Maggie."

"You're right, we all will."It seemed obvious to me that Maggie had the knack of captivating everybody she meets which should take her far in this world.

"I agree, I agree."

"You're not reading my thoughts now, are you?"

"I don't know what I'm doing, sometimes I just think the same as you, I think it's when you're thinking about Maggie, that's all."

Caz came and stood next to me.

"Have you any idea what she's now worth?" She looked shocked.

"Well I know it's a lot, but I don't know how much."

"She is worth millions, billions in fact, plus houses, hotels,

154

she even owns a bloody island in the Caribbean."

I couldn't help but laugh, she was so shocked. What a weight to carry, I thought, for a young kid.

She'll need all the help we can get her and give her.

"Right," said Jimmy, "let's get back to work, time's getting short."

They turned immediately and got down to it.

"What did he mean about time getting short?" asked Sarah.

"I've laid a trail for Lord Nigel, hopefully leading him to believe that we are all due to meet at my office at four.

That's what all the airport changes and phone calls were about.

I wanted to give us a bit of time to get all the wills and paperwork sorted and official before the Lord catches up to us. Hopefully he will realise that he's lost by then and give up the desire to kill Maggie." I went on to explain that if Maggie had not turned up to claim her inheritance it automatically reverted to Nigel.

"So he needed to kill Maggie before she got to the lawyers and claimed it?"

"That's right and he's lost that, so let's hope he has enough control of his behaviour to realise that and give it up. We don't know how far gone he is, but we do know he is an extremely dangerous man."

There was an extended pause before Sarah spoke.

"If that's the right word? Right so what if Nigel still kills Maggie, what happens then?"

"Well," I said, "we have given that a lot of thought and what we came up with is as follows."

I noticed that Maggie and Caz were listening intently to the conversation without questioning who I was talking to. Jimmy just looked puzzled.

"If he has lost the plot completely and kills Maggie, he would then have to go and kill whoever is her beneficiaries before they can lay claim to the will, also anyone who was a witness to all this. He would need to get away with all this to stand any chance of benefiting. I can't see how he could possibly think this could happen, but who knows how his mind is working, so we had to plan just in case."

"So what did you plan?""I'll tell you later when it's all in place."

At that moment there was a knock on the door, everybody turned in alarm and faced the door. Bill was already behind the door with his gun in his hand. Jimmy opened the office door.

"Don't worry, I've got some couriers due, so don't shoot them until you're sure."

I opened the door somewhat tentatively, there was a lad of about seventeen. "Courier for a Mr Carmichael."

"Take your helmet off and come in," I said.

Removing his motorcycle helmet, he stepped through the door. I think he saw Bill putting his gun back in its holster, because next time he spoke he sounded very shaken.

"Is Mr Carmichael here?" he asked. I think it was crossing his mind whether or not to make a run for it.

At that moment Jimmy burst through the office door.

"Billy," he said, which settled poor Billy straight away.

"Hello sir, thank god it's you, I was getting a bit poutie round the old arris, I don't mind telling you."Jimmy had four A4-sized envelopes in his hands, which he handed to Billy. "Now you know where these have got to go, don't you Billy?"

"Sure I do," said Billy very sure now, having got over his initial fright.

Jimmy showed him out the door, tapped him on the back and said, "There will be a bonus for you when this is all over

Bill." He waved him off and closed the door.

"What was all that poutie business?" asked Caz.

"That was slang, meaning he was scared, it's taken me six months to stop him saying 'innit', at the end of every sentence. He's a good lad, is Billy, I've got big plans for him."

Caz whispered to me, "What's all that 'innit' business about?"

"Don't worry darling, they wouldn't have taught that at Roedean." She punched me and walked back into the office with Maggie and Jimmy.

We sat for about another half hour, getting more tense with every minute that passed. The knock on the door sounded like an explosion in the silence. I opened it and Bill was once again positioned behind the door. It was Billy. "Only me chief," he said. This time he took a sneaky look behind the door to verify he was right the first time.

"Billy this is Bill." They nodded, at least Bill hadn't taken his gun out this time.

"I've got to see Mr Jimmy quick."

Jimmy had just opened the door and was coming through when he saw Billy. "Good lad Billy, we've just about finished."

"There's something I've got to tell yer first Mr J., someone tried to follow me."

I jumped up at that. "Who? How do you know it was you they were following?"

Billy looked at me with something approaching contempt.

Jimmy spoke. "If Billy says someone tried to follow him, you can be certain it's true, believe me."

"What did he look like, Billy?"

"Old, dark hair, driving a posh car, even took the reg no." He passed us a piece of paper.

"It's Nigel," I said.

"But Nigel's not old," said Maggie. "Billy, this old guy

was he my age or the inspector's?"

"More like yours, like I said," answered Billy. Billy was seventeen and anyone over thirty was old to him.

"So it's Nigel." Everyone nodded. "Did he follow you here?" "NO, of course not, I lost him then drove around a bit to make sure, before coming here.""Good lad."I had picked up on Jimmy's confidence in Billy and was sure he had lost his pursuers.

Billy had lived on the London streets all his life, I shouldn't think anyone would get one over on him on his home turf.

Jimmy had another four envelopes ready for Billy.

"Right Billy, you know where these have got to go, I'm relying on you to make sure they get there."

"You leave it to me Mr J." And he was gone.

Everybody was seated now catching up on food and drink, Caz sat next to me.

I looked at the wound on her cheek and was overcome with a wave of guilt. I had been so engrossed in my plans, I had virtually ignored the fact that not only my wife, but a whole load of people very close to me had been close to death, some were still in hospital, being treated.

"Tell me all that has happened."

"Look David, none of it was your fault, I know what you're thinking but it wasn't. We all knew what could happen and would do it without question again. You're not the only one who wants to fight and beat this lot, just remember that."

She then for the next twenty minutes related the whole story, finishing up with "Then Bill shot him and saved me and John, but John told everyone it was me, because of Bill's previous with them."

I looked at Bill. "Thanks mate."

"No need," he said. "One of the best moments of the last few years."

I think being able to gain revenge without being locked up had truly made him a happy man, but I will always be grateful that he was there when we needed him.

Jimmy's voice – "We had better get going" – brought us back to the present and the next step of our plan.

"You're right, Maggie and Caz you had better stay here with Jenny." Jenny was a WPS. From the protection squad.

"Just in case he was to come here."

"Don't be bloody silly." It was Maggie and she looked angry.

"I'm not staying here, he is expecting me at your offices, right?"

I nodded.

"Well if he's watching and spots you going in without me, your plan is shot, he will know something is up and will start looking for me elsewhere, starting here I should think. Well, am I right?"

I couldn't argue, she was of course perfectly right.

"OK," I said, "you go with us."

Within minutes we were on our way to my office.

"I'm sorry I shouted in there, but I knew I was right, I know you were just trying to keep me safe, but all those people trying to help me, I couldn't hide away while you all took the risks, could I?"I shook my head.

"I just feel guilty about all these people getting hurt because of me and wanted to keep you out of the firing line now we are so close to the end."

"I know we are close to the finish now, but we've got to beat him together, OK uncle David?"

She tried her best to repress a grin.

"I'm sure she's flirting."

CHAPTER TWENTY-ONE (YES OR NO)

We went quiet for the few minutes it took to reach my office. We pulled into our small car park and climbed from the car. There were five of us in all, Inspector Charlie, Bill Meeks, Maggie, Jimmy and of course me. I haven't mentioned Sarah, but she was there somewhere, I hoped.

We entered the offices then up in the lift to my floor, the building was only three floors but we all used the lift. We walked into the empty office, I turned on the lights and started turning all the computers on.

"Why are you doing that?" said Jimmy.

"I can't stand empty offices, there's something strange about them." Nobody contradicted me, perhaps it wasn't just me! We all took seats and waited apprehensively.

"It's about time, isn't it?" said the inspector.

I nodded.

"David." It was Sarah. **"Something is wrong."**

"What?""I don't know for sure but I feel it, something is wrong in this building. I still don't understand this spooky stuff, but I know what I feel and I'm very sure."

I've grown to trust her feelings and this was no different.

"He's probably in the building," I said this out loud, everyone turned to face me.

"What makes you think that?" someone asked.

"I've just got a feeling."

Of course they were not privy to my conversation with Sarah.

Bill and the inspector had their guns out checking them. The silence was broken by my phone ringing, I leaned over and lifted it.

"Hello."

"David dear boy." There was no mistaking who it was. "I want you to listen to me, do not speak. In fact put your phone on speaker, I want everyone to hear."

I pressed the button and announced to the rest, "It's Nigel."

They sat forward.

"It's Lord Nigel, but I'll forget your attempt to irritate me for the moment. Is everybody paying attention?"

"Yes," I answered.

"Right, I am in the building and I have Mrs Hollins right alongside me, do you understand?" My mind was buzzing, this was the error, I knew there would be one, I had left Caz with just one policewoman that was our weak point.

"Sarah?"

"I've checked, he's just outside the lift, he's got your wife with a gun to her head."

"Don't wait out there, your lordship, come in."

There was silence, probably he was looking round for a camera to explain how I seemed to know where he was.

"He's coming," said Sarah.

"Come in Nigel, the door is open."

The door opened, not fully but enough so he could see in.

"Right, firstly Mr Densil and Mr Meeks put your weapons in the waste basket by the window."

They didn't move. "Unless you want me to shoot the lovely Caroline, you surely can't have any doubts that I will do it."

Charlie and Bill looked towards me, they didn't have to ask the question, I nodded.

"Do as he asks," I said.

"NOW!" he shouted from the door.

They moved to the basket by the window, placed the guns in and then sat back down. The door opened a bit more so we could see Caz but just an outline of Nigel.

"Now David, you put your gun on the table, and I will search everyone and should I find a weapon I will kill whoever."

I placed my gun on the desk. "Could you take the gun from my wife's head now, we've done as you asked, and for god's sake stop hiding in the doorway, come in and we can talk about your grievances."

He moved into the room but kept Caz between him and us. Moving a chair for her to sit on and one for himself behind so he was partially obscured, should anyone attempt a shot.

"Your reputation goes before you my friend, you and your friends have killed a great many of my employees."

"Only in self defence as you well know," I said.

"That is a matter of opinion, it's a shame that the sergeant major's not here, I could settle that score anyway."

"You mean the old man you don't have to worry about?"

His eyes darkened and I thought maybe I had pushed him too far, with him holding a gun to my wife's head and us unarmed.

"Anyway Sir Nigel, please relax, let's talk."

I think he was getting confident now he seemed less tense.

I couldn't help thinking if John were here and saw him threatening Caz with a gun, even if he emptied the chamber into him, John would still have got to him, got his hands round his throat and refuse to die before finishing him off.

"Right," he said,

"why do you assume I'm too late? When you don't even know what my objectives are?"

I thought I had had to try to convince him before Charlie or Bill thought they were John and went for him, they might be good but nobody came close to John.

"I'll be perfectly honest with you about your objectives, you want control of the group, why? Because you are just about to float it on the markets, you could sell a good portion of the shares, making you untold billions, giving you the capital to expand as you wish, and still retain overall control. How am I doing so far?""Not bad, but how am I too late? Even assuming she has claimed her inheritance, can she prove she's his daughter? Is there a birth certificate? It's not at all clear."

He knew better, if indeed he was going to contest the fact that she was indeed his father's child, he couldn't argue with the fact that Sarah's will left everything to her daughter, plus the time it would take made it a non-starter for him.

Sarah piped up,

"Not only is there a birth certificate, his father was sent a copy via his solicitors, so he knew and accepted the fact."

I relayed these facts to Nigel, which shook him. I think perhaps he knew but couldn't understand how anyone else could possibly know.

He paused for a moment. "That makes it easier, I just shoot her and I feel it would all come back to me as her brother and head of the family, also CEO of the company."

I looked to Jimmy, who noticed and took up the next chapter. "Well Sir Nigel, I will explain the predicament you find yourself in. Lady Margaret, I'm sure if you can be a sir, she can be a lady." Nigel's face had reached a shade I'd never seen before, on anybody still alive that is, but it had given me the opportunity to release my knife from my jacket. What I would do, I hadn't yet planned, but in the next few minutes, Nigel would either admit defeat, or would lose control and try to kill everyone he blamed for his situation. None of us knew, especially Nigel.

Jimmy continued without the slightest sign of fear. "As I was saying, Lady Margaret has taken the precaution of making a will of her own, and bearing in mind your liking for violence, has made her plans accordingly." "So who has she left it to?"

Nigel was still cocky but his confidence was definitely beginning to fade.

Jimmy stood up and walked over to Nigel who raised his gun to point it straight at Jimmy's chest. "You'll like this dear boy," said Jimmy straight into Nigel's face.

Now I could see Jimmy was being deliberately provocative, I assumed he thought I was up to something and he was trying to take all the attention away from me. Please Jimmy, be careful, but Jimmy was in full swing now and nothing could stop him.

"I'll carry on."

It had done the trick, everyone's eyes were on him, transfixed.

"This is how it works, old boy. On the demise of Lady Margaret, her estate, lock, stock and barrel goes into a trust, which is shared equally between five, yes five hundred charities, assuming that every charity has a board of probably a dozen that means you would have to deal with some six thousand tree huggers, ninety per cent of whom will have no experience of business whatsoever. The very thought of it makes me feel like ending it all, what a wonderfully disgusting thing to do and all my own idea, don't thank me!"

I looked at Nigel. I thought for sure he was going to kill him just for the fun of it, his index finger was white on the trigger. I had the knife ready but I needed to get nearer to give me more chance. I knew I could get him but would I be able to without taking a bullet? I didn't think so.

There was no reason for him to kill Jimmy, but reality was not in Nigel's mind, just a desire to kill.

I swear I could see his trigger finger start to squeeze. "Wait a minute," said Nigel.

"I have a solution, you draft a new will naming me."

Jimmy smiled. "Then you have to kill everyone here, dispose of us, so we will never be found, then make sure Lady Margaret's death is an accident or natural causes. Do you think all that is possible? I don't think so, plus the new will has only been registered this afternoon, do you think the authorities are not going to find a new will within hours extremely suspicious?"

Jimmy was obviously playing for time, hoping I would be able to do whatever I was planning and quick. The whole scheme was bizarre, but perhaps in Nigel's strange brain, feasible. I was still, edging nearer, each inch giving me hopefully a better chance of my knife getting to him before his bullets can get to me. I knew I would get to him, once I made my move nothing would stop me, but would I be quick enough to survive and kill him before he could reciprocate. I was not the man I was, but he had never been a soldier. I was not frightened but I just wanted to be sure that I could save those around me, let's hope so."Perhaps I should shoot a couple of people to show how ruthless I am," said Nigel.

Jimmy strode backwards and forwards across the office, I never realised he saw himself as Alec Guinness until now.

"What you don't realise your lordship is, I come from five hundred years of aristocracy, so therefore I don't give a shit who you shoot, and will not be impressed by such actions, we are only impressed by reward. You must have encountered this in your commercial enterprises, should you reward me as I feel I should be rewarded I will gladly take the gun and shoot them myself."

Bloody hell, that Jimmy was good, everybody was transfixed even Nigel smiled, he obviously did have experience of such people. NOT that I'm afraid of Jimmy's family, I knew his dad well, he was a bus driver in South London, but even I was inclined to believe he was for real. I hope he wasn't! I only needed a couple more feet and I might have a chance of killing him without my demise. Nigel wasn't sure whether he believed Jimmy or not, but I think he wanted to believe that other members of society were as devoid of a conscience as himself.

"You Maggie, go to the bin by the window and take out a gun, give it to him." He pointed to Jimmy.

"We'll see if he can kill, remember one wrong move and I start shooting."

What on earth was going on in Nigel's brain, his actions were getting more and more mad every minute. I would have to go soon, before we run out of time.

Maggie moved to the bin without hesitation, she bent and took a gun in her hand. I looked to Nigel, his grip on Caz had loosened just a bit, but that might be all I needed. I knew that once I moved there was no turning back, he would be dead, that I could guarantee, but would I? I stood up with the pretence of negotiating with Nigel, his gun moved to Caz's head again.

"Can't we at least talk? You know full well that you can't kill anyone here and get away with it. You're a billionaire, why on earth would you want more?"

"It's not the money, you fool, it's my company, I took it from my father and made it what it is today, nobody will ever take it away from me."

Everyone could now see the extent of his insanity, his eyes were bulging, veins sticking out, almost foaming at the mouth, he was completely off in his own world, reality didn't exist. It was obvious that we would get nowhere trying to talk. It was down to me and my knife. I sat down trying to look dejected, but I had gained another metre, maybe.

Maggie was in front of him with the gun by her side.

"Give the gun to James." Did he seriously think Jimmy would shoot anyone?"NO!" she said loudly, taking a step forward. "This must end now. I'm your family, are you really going to shoot me? You can have it all, I've never wanted it, it's yours."

His gun came up. It was aimed straight at her heart. My god he's going to do it.

"SHE'S YOUR DAUGHTER."

Sarah had somehow managed to articulate her emotion, it was a loud sort of roar, which absolutely worked. The whole room stood still in shock. I suppose I moved first because I knew what it was, therefore was not quite paralysed by shock. I sprang towards Nigel, the knife in my right hand, my left hand reached for Caz's shoulder or wherever I could touch.

I felt my hand touch her, I threw her as hard as I could just to get her safe out of the line of fire.

I couldn't think about her being hurt by my actions, I was desperate. She literally flew across the office crashing into all sorts of equipment with a wide-eyed look of shock on her face. God, I hope I hadn't hurt her. Once she was clear, I proceeded with my real target, Nigel.

This was a fraction of a second, but seemed like forever. Everybody was still static as I grabbed Nigel's gun hand just as he started to move, I pulled him towards me putting him off balance.

The knife was already moving towards its target when I heard him fire. I was holding his hand down by my side to stop him shooting anyone, I felt a fierce burning all down my left side.

I still felt OK and the knife was still moving, I felt the blade press against his ribs, I braced myself for the final thrust. My arm was now round his neck still holding his gun hand, my other hand moving forward with the knife. It would be over in a second now.

"Please David." I felt her hand on my shoulder. I looked round to see Maggie.

"He is my family, please don't let it end like this, there has been too much killing."

I looked from her back to Nigel, he just seemed like a broken pathetic nothing. I think Sarah's outburst had finally killed something in him, perhaps the hatred had just drained.

I don't know, but looking at him now you could not see why he had engendered such fear, he was broken.

I withdrew the knife and took the gun. I noticed, as did Maggie, the blood on the end of the blade.

"You nearly did it," she said. "I wanted to," I answered.

"Thank you, David," she said and put her arms round my neck.

The room was beginning to come to life now, everyone recovering from the shock of the last few minutes.

CHAPTER TWENTY-TWO
(THE AFTERMATH)

Charlie and Bill retrieved their guns and were handcuffing Nigel. Caz was struggling to pick herself up from where I had thrown her, I rushed to her side.

"I'm so sorry darling, I just needed you safe."

"I know that, but I'm not sure the baby does."

There was silence, Maggie was grinning, even Jimmy and the two burly cops were still in their tracks.

"Are you telling me …?"

"Yes I am and don't ask me how or I'll thump you."

The police arrived out front, the inspector handed him over and he was heading off to the station and it was just me, Caz and Maggie. We were all shattered.

"Is it over?" said Maggie.

"It is, isn't it David?" said Caz.

"Well I think it is and we are still all alive aren't we?"

"David." It was Sarah.

"Thank you darling."

"It's fine, we love her just like you do. Why are you still here? You were supposed to go once it was over."

"Bloody charming, I don't know what is going to happen so don't ask."

"Are you talking to Mum?" I nodded.

"Is she happy?"

"Yes she's really happy," I said over some mumbling in the background from Sarah.

The three musketeers came back in just as we were having a hug.

"He's gone to be charged and to be seen by a doctor. He's got a cut on his chest, but mostly, mentally he needs attention. What about you? He fired the gun straight at you, point blank."

"I remember the burning sensation, I pulled my jacket open, my left side was covered in blood."

"Oh my god," said Maggie and Caz in unison, pulling at my shirt.

I looked down. I had a flash burn down my left side and a bullet had scored across my ribs, I knew it was not serious but the two women tending to me were not listening.

"You must go to hospital," they said in unison yet again.

"I will if you will," I said to Caz.

"Just to check."

I had a feeling this was a portent of things to come with two women looking after my well-being, whether I liked it or not.

"Just one thing."

I don't know who it was but I knew it was coming.

"What did we just witness?" said Jimmy, the others nodding. "The ghostly voice, please don't tell us you're a bloody ventriloquist, we all know what we heard."

"Tell them to piss off or I'll haunt them."

"Christ, are you still here?""Look my friends, I will tell it all but not right now, I will write the whole story and send you all a copy. But at the moment I think we had better get to the hospital."

They looked at me rather strange, but I think they realised it was all they were going to get. I needed to sort things out in my own head before I could try and explain to others.

So off we went to the hospital where Caz had a scan and general check over. Maggie and I just cried when they gave us a picture of something that resembled a peanut we decided much to Caz's displeasure.

After they finished with Caz, I let them tend to me. By this time the department was full of policemen, with armed officers on every entrance/exit.

When the doctor looked at my side, she knew straight away it was a gunshot wound. I don't think they were sure if we were heroes or serial killers.

The inspector I assume told them, because we were treated very well from then on, from what I can remember.

Within half an hour I was out, being operated on. I had a couple of broken ribs, flash burns and a wound across my side, nothing too serious but they wouldn't let me home for a few days.

Six months or so later, Joshua arrived without complication, the only problem was fighting Mum and auntie Maggie to get any time with him, but we managed.

So it was during one of my moments with Josh in the bath that the dark thoughts reappeared to invade my subconscious, they had been around for some time but I managed to cope with them. They seem to be back with a vengeance since I became a father and playing with my son.

The door opened, in came Caz and Maggie giggling and armed with a camera.

"What on earth …" I started to say.

Maggie started to click away.

"We just thought we'd take some pictures for Josh for when he grows up," said Caz. "Him and his psycho killer dad."

She knew then! Why would I be surprised, she always knew what I was thinking.

"Let's just see the damage that your kill-crazy dad has done to those that rely on him and love him even. Starting with our little Maggie."

"I would be dead without you, you can't argue with that," interrupted Maggie.

"How does Mum feel about what you've done?"

"Mike and Sammie are now married and expecting because of you and your protection and planning, don't you know they love you?

Bill Meeks' life has been turned around because you were willing to stand and fight, he thinks you're God."

"What about John?"

"John has learned through his lifetime not to worry about things, he just does what he thinks is right and that's enough for him, so he's fine."

"Finally, that little bundle you're holding wouldn't have a daddy to play in the bath with if you hadn't fought back, so please stop thinking too much and start appreciating what you've got, and I hope you'll always be prepared to stand up and fight for us,"

"She's right, you know."

"Christ, you're back."

"Hello Sarah," said the girls in unison.

"Right," I said, "this is like being in a girls netball team changing room." I passed Josh to his mum.

"It's OK," said Maggie. "Don't worry about the photos, we'll tell everyone the water was very cold." And she collapsed in laughter.

"That's it!" I shouted, "you are going in the bath and I'll have my own photos."

I started to rise, Maggie screamed and ran.

"You could scar that poor child for life," said Caz as I put my arm round her.

"What about me?" I asked.

"You're OK now aren't you?"

"Yes," I answered.

"I just worry that Josh will inherit too many of my genes, that's all."

"Listen you, I hope to god he inherits plenty of your genes, just as long as he gets plenty of mine to help him obtain perfection."

CHAPTER TWENTY-THREE (FINALE)

It is now some fourteen months since Nigel was arrested. I had naively thought that would be more or less the end of the saga, unfortunately it didn't quite work out like that.

There were the endless police interviews, statement after statement, and of course there was the press. It was a major story, a multimillionaire, titles, a lost daughter, a murdered wife and of course sex. It had all the ingredients of a Jeffrey Archer novel and the public couldn't get enough of it. I tried to be fair to the press, they had helped us when we needed it, and of course I was one of them, however much I would at times like to deny it.

The Special Branch or MI5, or at least one of the spook branches, was giving me a hard time for quite a while.

A list of bodies from my house, people missing in Spain, falsifying flight plans, then you attempted to stab Lord Benson. I explained to them that I was out of the country when my house was attacked, I had no knowledge of people in Spain disappearing.

I had intended to fly to Italy as per my flight plan, but due to a bit of engine trouble I had decided to land at a friend's farm in Spain instead, just to be safe.

As for Lord Benson, how could I have – attempted – to stab him? He was in my control, I had the knife in my hand, I could as you know, have killed him in an instant, had that been my intention. They were well aware of my past by this time, so was everybody else. So to infer that I 'attempted' to stab him was bullshit and they knew it.

"I suppose there was a fault with your radio, that stopped

you reporting all this and explaining to the authorities here."

I nodded, they obviously didn't believe me, they knew I'd been up to something, but couldn't figure out what, as yet.

John then made his allowed phone call, after making a few threats, who or where he called, I've no idea, but a short while later a tall spooky looking man at the department showed his ID and wagged his finger at the police. They looked distinctly uncomfortable, but they didn't argue, they just shook his hand and showed him out. They had a little conference amongst themselves, then came to talk with us. They were all smiles. There were to be no charges against us and we were free to go. John gave me a little wink, we all shook hands with the police and left. I never asked who he phoned but hopefully one day he'll tell me.

The furore had started to calm down, We were hoping to get back to some sort of normality when the trial date was announced, and so it started all over again, but even worse.

We had sat down with Maggie when the question of her father had first been raised in my office; seems like a lifetime ago now. I told her that her mum and I had gone over what had happened all those years ago.

It appears that she and Nigel did have a brief affair, she never tried to excuse what had happened, she just said that she and Nigel were left alone for long periods of time, with Gordon away much of the time. Although she insists that she loved Gordon, she was young and very lonely and of course Nigel was much nearer her age.

"Well it just bloody happened, what can I say?"

When she found out she was pregnant she was sure Gordon was the father and she still is today. But things between her and Gordon had begun to sour for her within their relationship. She knew what Gordon was capable of, she had an overwhelming fear that when the truth came out, and she was sure it would, Nigel would make sure of that. Gordon would just take the baby and she would be left. They were in love, she was pretty sure of that, but Gordon was, as she knew, a hard man, used to being boss and getting his own way. She had no doubt how he would react.

Although she thought she had bought all this on herself, she knew what the future would be and it wasn't good. After many sleepless nights she made up her mind; if she wanted to keep her baby, which was what she wanted more than anything, she would have to disappear. How, she did not know, but she knew that if she wanted to avoid being out on the streets and never see her baby, it was her only option.

So although not much more than a kid herself, she was to prove more than a match for those she was frightened of, the rest you know.

Maggie looked at me as I related the facts, she never needed to think at all, she just looked me in the eyes and said, "I really don't care very much who my father may or may not be – I had the right mother!"

"How did I get a daughter like that?"

I felt she could take a great deal of credit for Maggie. She had, as we know, been the overwhelming influence for the whole of her life, this was beyond dispute and knowing what we now know she had saved her and kept her alive for all those years, but I said nothing.

Now we had to settle the next problem.

"Maggie, you know that you have to get a DNA test done."I could feel her hackles rise.

"Why? I don't care so what's the point?".

"The thing is, that's OK you don't care, but you know there are already rumours about what happened to us that day in the office and it won't stop at rumours. Someone will find out the truth, or their version of the truth and you will be pilloried for it. Can you imagine the headlines? Lurid stories about a ménage à trois.

Stories about your being a witness against your own father, the crimes will be forgotten, it will just be about you and your mum. The family, things you have no idea about, once it starts it takes on a life of its own, believe me I know what I'm talking about."

She thought for a moment and then said,

"OK, arrange it."

The test was done, with a lot of string pulling it wouldn't be more than a few days until we got the results.

In the meantime, Maggie continued to visit Nigel. I felt uneasy about it, so did Sarah. We felt that it inevitably would only lead to problems. He was obviously charming her and she was a willing subject, like most psychopathic personalities they can be and usually are, very devious and manipulative.

I didn't know what I could do to resolve the situation, but fate was about to step in and yet again lend a helping hand. I had a result from the lab on the DNA, well it wasn't a definitive result, it appears that the bloodline was so close it was difficult for them to give a definite answer. They did say when I pushed them for an answer, that they thought it most likely that Gordon was her dad. This information was just for me, to go to a court of law would need much more in depth test to be certain.

I told Maggie that it looked highly likely that Gordon was her father, but there was some doubt because of the closeness. She seemed to accept this. I truly believe that she had no interest in who her father was.

It wasn't more than half an hour after Maggie left that I received the call. I picked up the phone and spoke.

"Hello, David Hollins."

It was the prison trying to contact Maggie.

"She's not here at present, I'm her guardian, can I help?"

"I suppose I can tell you sir, it's Nigel Benson, I'm afraid he's dead."

"How?" I more or less gasped.

"There was nothing wrong with his health surely?"

"It appears to have been a revenge attack, we had heard rumours, that is why we had him segregated. It seems he went to the laundry to get clean sheets for his wing, someone was lying in wait. He opened the door, walked in with an armful of old sheets, whoever was waiting stabbed him. Evidently he used a ballpoint pen sharpened to a point, with a cross piece to form a 'T', thrust it straight into his eye, it penetrated about five inches right into his brain, he was dead in minutes. The perpetrator has disappeared for the moment, but we will catch whoever it was." I replaced the phone and leaned back in my chair, I didn't care who had done the deed I thought, it just seemed inevitable that someone would. You spend your whole life making enemies, sooner or later one of them will try to take revenge.

In most lives of course it wouldn't be a sharp object rammed into your brain via your eyeball, but if you have enemies they are always waiting to take revenge in one form or the other. I wonder if Nigel had known he was in danger? It probably never entered his head that he had ever done anything wrong to anyone.

The phone startled me from my thoughts.

"Hello, Dave Hollins."

It was Winchester Prison again. It appeared that Maggie had arrived at the prison since their previous call and they were unsure how I wanted it handled.

"Listen, if you can delay telling her for a while, I will leave for the prison now, I should be there in about half an hour, so if you have to tell her, let her know that I'm on my way and will be there in a few minutes."

"OK sir, leave it to me, we will look after her until you arrive."

I thanked him, put the phone down and left. I made it in twenty minutes.

She was in a little office, sitting alone, huddled up on a chair. I saw her before she noticed me. I looked at her and thought she had lost about eight of her years; she seemed like a small child. I could see where the tears had run down her cheeks. It would not have surprised me to see her sucking her thumb.

She spotted me, ran towards me and let her emotions loose.

I just held her until she had let out what she needed to.

My phone rang, it was Caz. "Hello." "I just heard, how's Maggie?"

"She's devastated, she's not spoken yet, just cried." "David, just bring her home to me."

I knew then once and for all that she was ours. Caz and Maggie had experienced no supernatural experiences, they just loved each other, simple.

"OK."

I knew Sarah was with us as I put my phone away and put my arm around Maggie to help her up.

"That's it David, she needs her mother, take her home," said Sarah.

"How do you feel about that?"

"I feel good, of course it hurts but it's what I wanted from the minute I saw that car and knew I was going to die, someone to love and help Maggie. It appears I struck lucky. Maybe there was some divine help, I don't know, perhaps I like the idea. I just knew I could never go until she was safe. Not

just physically from Nigel but emotionally as well, I spent the last eighteen years without emotional happiness, it stops you from being complete, do you understand?"

"I do Sarah, you know me well enough to realise I was a troubled soul, only half a person until I met Cazzie, so I do know exactly what you mean and we will do everything we think you would want for her, she is after all you daughter."

"On the contrary David, she's yours now."

I took her home to Caz. They were in the bedroom for hours.

I heard them leave the bedroom. I sat apprehensively as they made their way down to the lounge, wondering what would be the consequences of what had happened.

The door opened and in walked Maggie. She looked radiant, back to the beautiful young woman again.

"Thank you David, I'm OK now."

I gave her a hug, then whispered to Caz, "What did you say?"

We moved to the kitchen where she busied herself making us all tea and sandwiches.

"Well?" I repeated.

"She got herself into such a state because she felt every member of her family were being killed, she was desperate to belong to someone, she's never felt that she was a part of anything."

"So what did you say?"

"Oh I just told her that we wanted to adopt her, then she'd have a brother and a second mum and dad.

Also, she has a family, Conway was her mum's maiden name, which sounds like it could be Irish therefore there could be loads of them."

"Of course, what did she make of that?"

"Well it seemed to work, didn't it?"

"You're bloody brilliant!"

"Thank you."

"Isn't she a bit old to be our little girl?"

"I thought she would like it, don't you?"

"What about Sarah?" "Why don't you ask me?"

"Well?" I enquired.

"If I had the choice I would have chosen to be with her forever, but that choice was taken from me. Bearing that in mind, I can't think of anybody

I'd choose before you and Caz to look after my lovely girl, so thank you and yes you have my blessing."

I nodded to Caz. "She's happy," I whispered.

"I've just had a thought, I wonder if you age here? Wherever I am, I could be an old wrinkly of about one hundred and fifty by the time I meet her again." Trust Sarah.

So here we are, I got to it and wrote the book. I had already done the first draft but there were unfinished issues with all of us which seemed to be resolving themselves.

Maggie has started university, studying business of course. There had been a brief romance between her and Carlos, they would now be apart for some time, so who knows for the future.

She had met her half brother and sister, they had got on like a house on fire, perhaps Nigel had an adverse effect on all those near to him. They certainly seem to have grown up since his demise, they were now quite pleasant.

Maggie had organised the long-awaited dinner for all those involved in our adventure, from the security guard at Popham airfield to Sir Michael Perry, who was doing a great job with Maggie's companies. They had been going from strength to strength under his stewardship. He was mentoring Maggie every spare minute she had, and he had already confided in me that she was a natural, in his opinion she would become widely renowned in the business world.

There was even a representative from AI international of Portsmouth, the company that developed God's Avenging Arm. Even little Billy the courier was there.

She had even found a way to reward everyone that had helped us in any way with our struggle. I had no idea until I started getting phone calls from a number of people enquiring about certain amounts of money that had appeared in their bank accounts unexplained, all they could trace was an international dealing company listing Sir Michael Perry as MD. I told them I would find out what I could but I was sure it was all above board and to hang on to it.

"Look Daddy, this is my decision, my money."I suppose that was the end of that, whose idea was it to adopt?"Concerning the financial rewards that you all have received," A murmur audibly travelled the tables where the remnants of the meal could still be seen.

I carried on. "If it was up to me of course you would have got bugger all, scruffy lot of adulterers, drunkards and god knows what else."

The room erupted in laughter and jeers.

"See, you prove my point." More noise.

I lifted my hands asking for silence. As it quietened down, I continued. "On a serious note however, I must offer you all a sincere thank you. I hope you have all read the book by now." I had sent them all a copy when it was first printed. "This was the easiest way for me to give you an explanation, I couldn't face trying to explain to you one by one. So thanks for all you did and thanks for coming.

"Thanks."

I received a small round of applause then the inevitable questions.

"What about Sarah, is she still around?"

"I haven't had any contact for months."And so it was to go on for some time. I think it ended up about fifty–fifty, those that believed and those that thought I'd invented a story to sell a book.

WHAT DO YOU THINK?

I walked to the entrance for some air and to gather my thoughts. It was a mild night, I sat on the steps thinking how lucky we had been with the outcome

"What about them not believing in me, bloody cheek."

"Oh you're bloody back."

"Yes, what about if I haunt them? I could tell you all their secrets, including the naughty bits, it could be your next book!"

"Sarah, shut up and don't you go anywhere near our friends."

"OK, I suppose this is it then."

"I think so sweetie, don't you?"

"Goodbye David, I love you."

"Bye, me too."

I WONDER!

ACKNOWLEDGEMENTS

Much of my research was of course done online. The company in Portsmouth that designed the sniper rifle is true, although it was actually designed for Arctic conditions, but it does still exist.

The Mafia deaths in Italy can all be verified and still go on to this day. In 2014, an official's son was kidnapped and murdered to stop his investigation into organised crime.

My most ardent thanks must go to a friend who I shall call Andy, who although is actually in the Australian forces somehow ended up training and working with our SAS. And like all special forces will not tell you how or why. When I showed him the outline of my story, he did let his guard down a bit, and I quote:

"If you knew of the things we got up to back then, both for your government and foreign (friendly) governments, with the regiment (SAS) and other units you would just not believe it mate, struth, looking back I don't know what was right or wrong. But your bloke has got right clearly on his side."

I wish now it had been that clear for us.

I think for soldiers this has always been a dilemma that they face; they do what they hope is right and maybe years later hopefully you find out it was.

But like us all, I like to think we can trust our forces, and I'm sure from what I know of them we can.

The character of Stanley who lives in Spain, is true. I can say no more to protect him and his wife's privacy, but as a well-known wildlife guide (worldwide) or if you are interested in birds especially birds of Andalusia, you already know him.

As for ghosts or the afterlife in any shape or form, I have no knowledge or expertise whatsoever, just my imagination.

I hope anyone who reads my book will enjoy it and the people in it, who are of course all real and completely true.

Well they are to me!